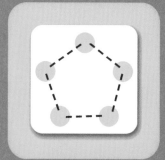

Jumbo Workbook

Come with me to learn about letters, numbers, and more!

D1328118

How to use this book

This book allows children to practice the skills that will help them for starting school and beyond.

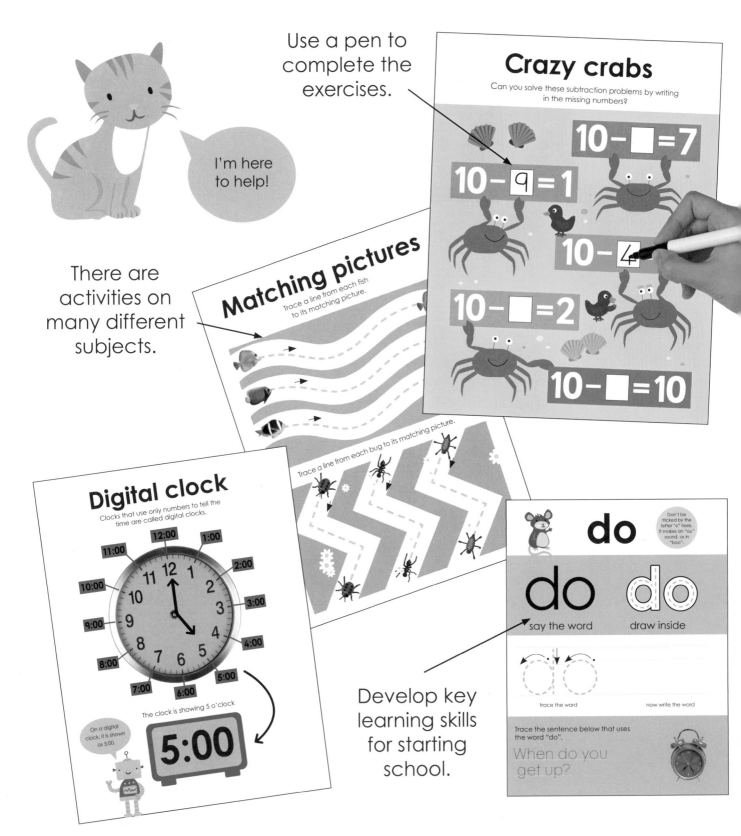

Use a pen to complete the exercises.

I'm here to help!

There are activities on many different subjects.

Crazy crabs

Can you solve these subtraction problems by writing in the missing numbers?

10 − ☐ = 7

10 − 9 = 1

10 − 4

10 − ☐ = 2

10 − ☐ = 10

Matching pictures

Trace a line from each fish to its matching picture.

Trace a line from each bug to its matching picture.

Digital clock

Clocks that use only numbers to tell the time are called digital clocks.

11:00 12:00 1:00
10:00 2:00
9:00 3:00
8:00 4:00
7:00 6:00 5:00

The clock is showing 5 o'clock

On a digital clock, it is shown as 5:00.

5:00

do

Don't be tricked by the letter "o" here. It makes an "ou" sound, as in "boo".

do   do

say the word   draw inside

trace the word   now write the word

Trace the sentence below that uses the word "do".

When do you get up?

Develop key learning skills for starting school.

Contents

Over 300 pages of fun-filled learning!

Pen Control

This section has simple tracing and pen control activities.

Down

Trace the dashed lines from top to bottom.

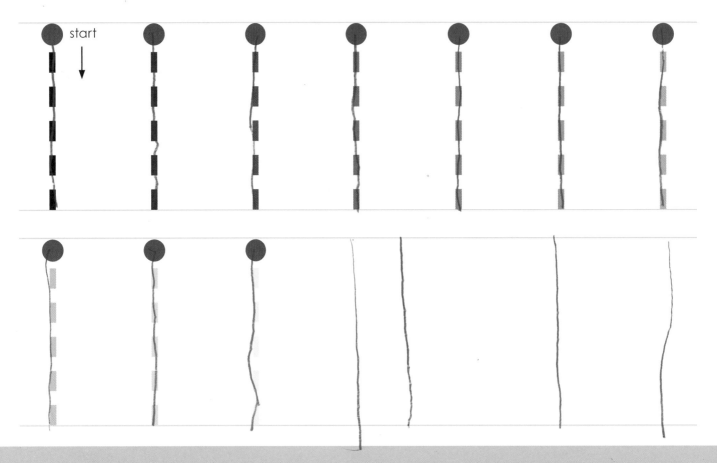

start

Can you trace the balloon strings from top to bottom?

start

Across

Follow the direction of the arrows.

Trace the dashed lines from left to right.

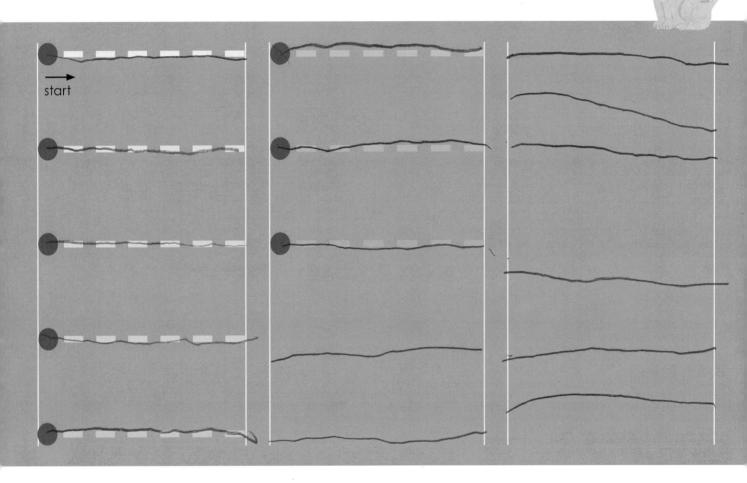

start

Can you trace along the arrows from left to right?

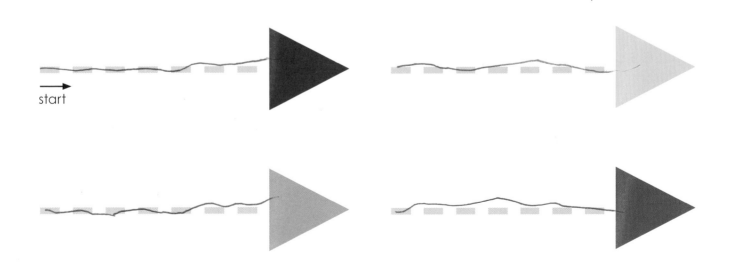

start

Diagonals

Try drawing them yourself!

Trace the dashed lines from top to bottom.

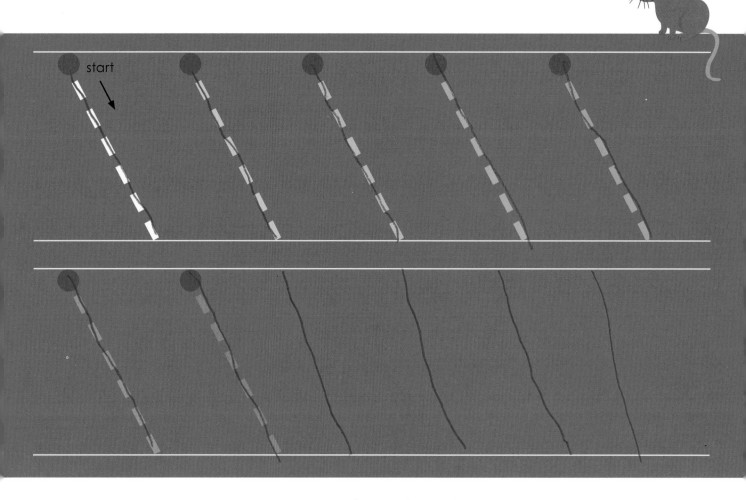

start

Can you trace along the kite strings from top to bottom?

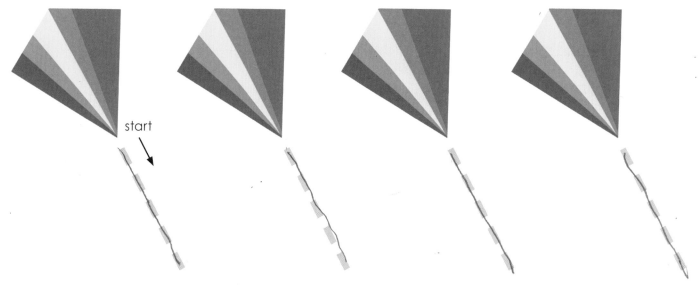

start

Curves

Trace the dashed lines down and around.

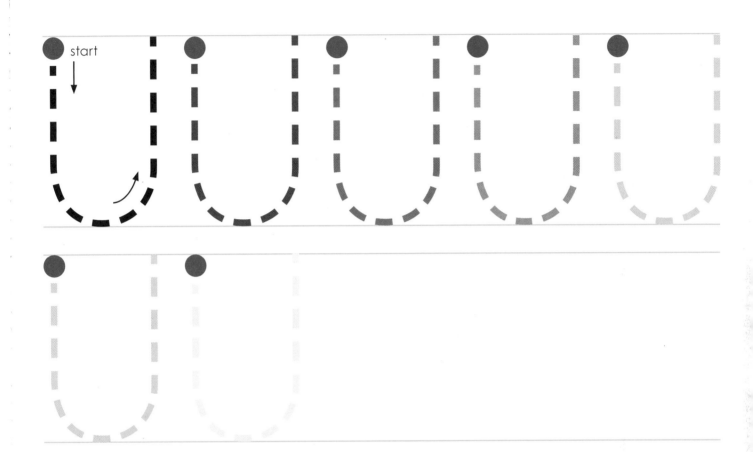

start

Can you trace the jump ropes down and around?

start

Straight line patterns

Can you trace the straight line patterns?

Now try drawing along these lines.

start ⟶

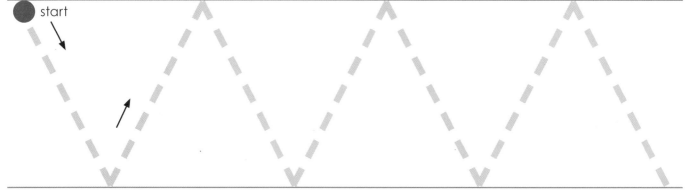

Curved line patterns

Can you trace the curved line patterns?

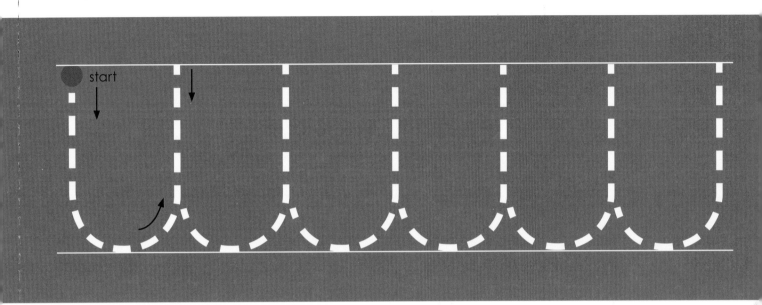

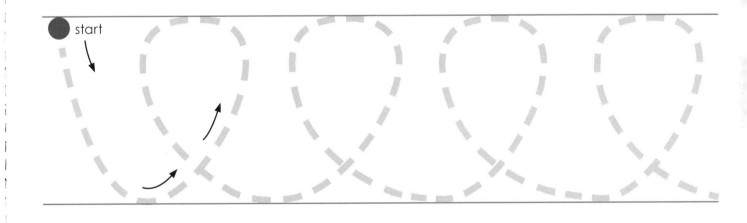

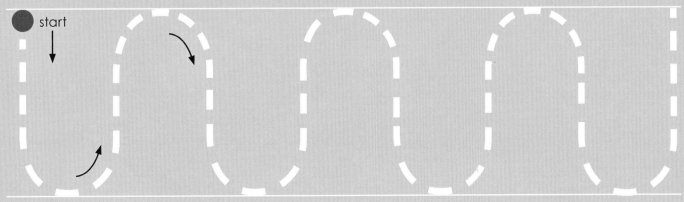

Matching pictures

Trace a line from each fish
to its matching picture.

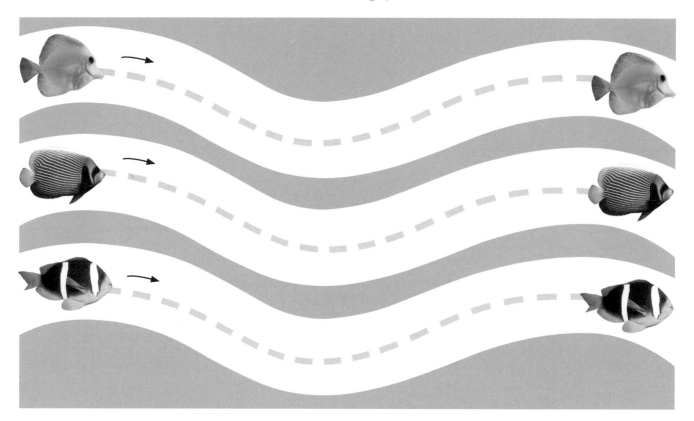

Trace a line from each bug to its matching picture.

Matching pictures

Trace a line from each rocket
to its matching picture.

Follow
the
arrows!

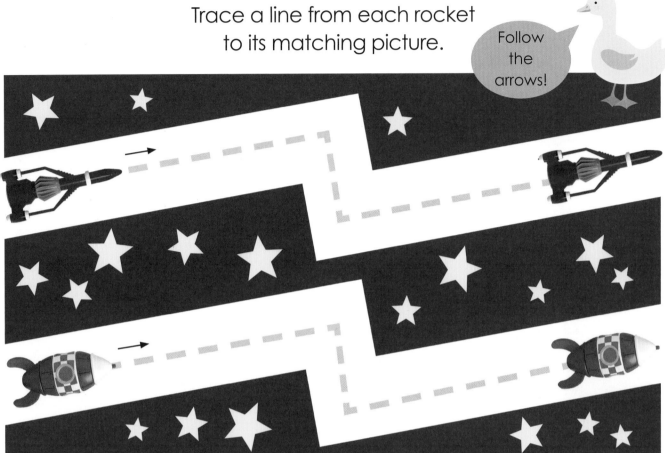

Trace a line from each vehicle to its matching picture.

Linking lines

Draw a line through all the apples
and oranges from start to finish.

start

This activity
has been
started for
you.

finish

Around and around

Trace over each swirl pattern.

start

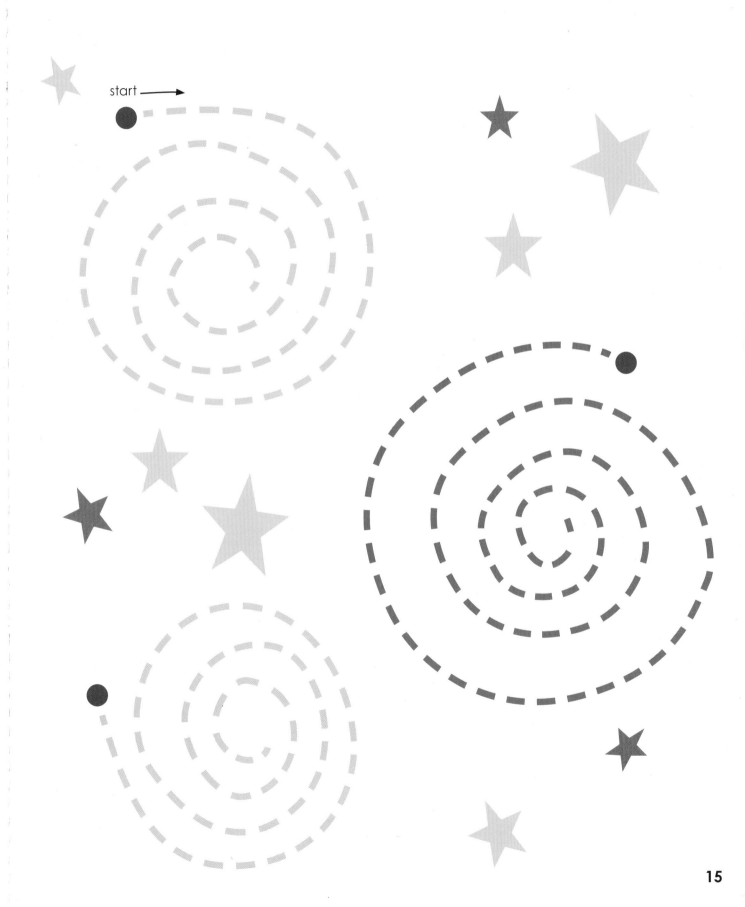

Squares

Look at the square

Trace the square

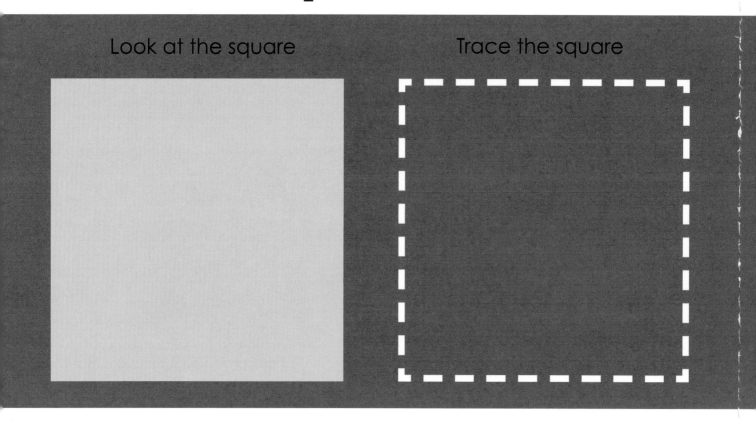

Can you trace these square-shaped things?

16

Ovals

Look at the oval

Draw the oval

Can you trace these oval-shaped things?

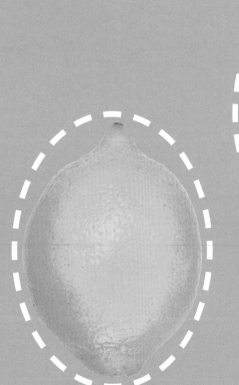

Circles

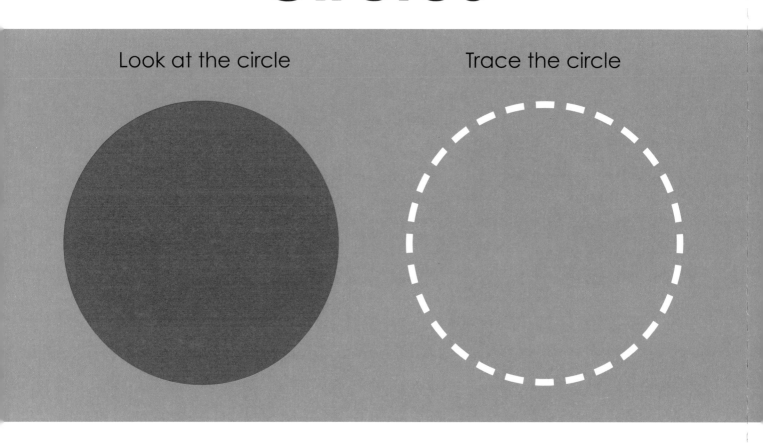

Look at the circle

Trace the circle

Can you trace these circular things?

Can you name all these things?

Triangles

Look at the triangle

Trace the triangle

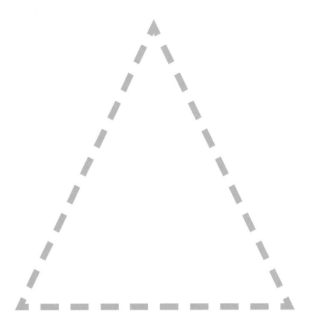

Can you trace these triangular things?

Rectangles

Look at the rectangle

Trace the rectangle

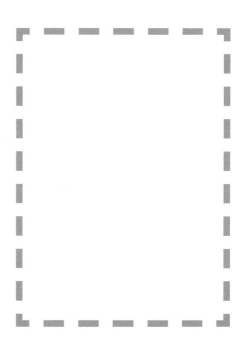

Can you trace these rectangular things?

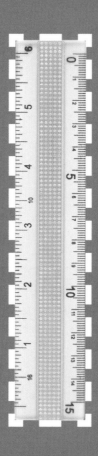

Hearts

Look at the heart

Trace the heart

Can you trace these heart-shaped things?

Follow the lines to trace the objects.

Diamonds

Look at the diamond

Trace the diamond

Can you trace these diamond-shaped things?

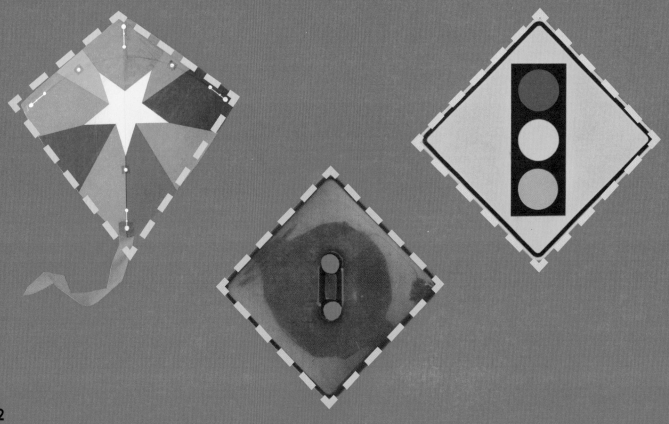

Stars

Stars can be tricky!

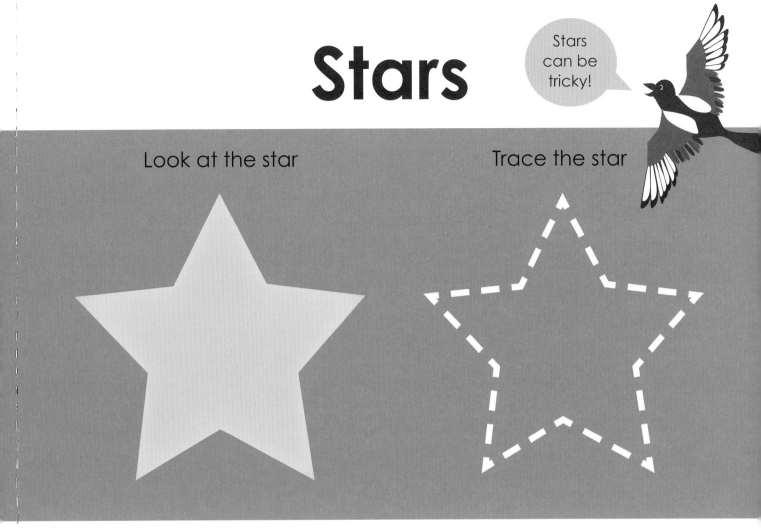

Look at the star

Trace the star

Can you trace these star-shaped things?

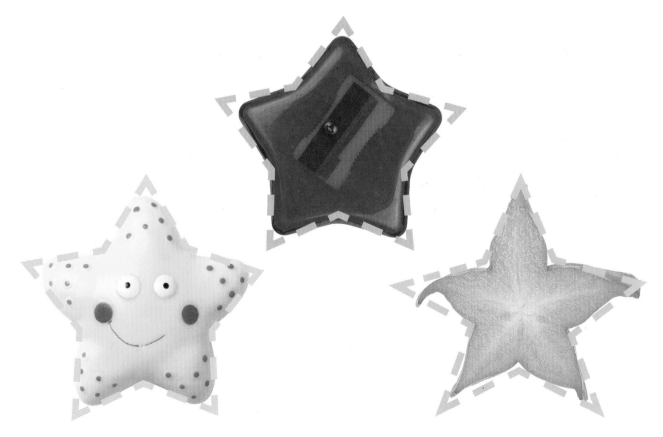

What's your favorite animal?

Pets

Look at the cat

Trace the cat's face

Look at the dog

Trace the dog's face

Insects

Look at the butterfly

Trace the butterfly

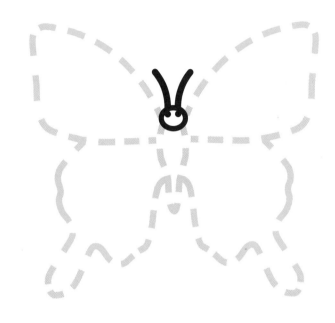

Look at the ladybug

Trace the ladybug

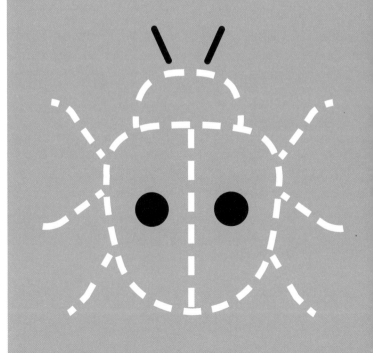

25

On the go

Look at the hot air balloon

Trace the hot air balloon

Look at the boat

Trace the boat

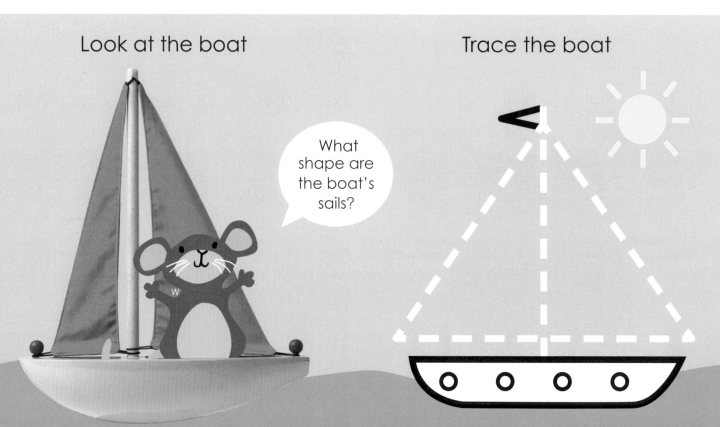

What shape are the boat's sails?

All about me

Look at the house

Trace the house

Look at the face

Trace the face

27

Nature

Look at the flower

Trace the flower

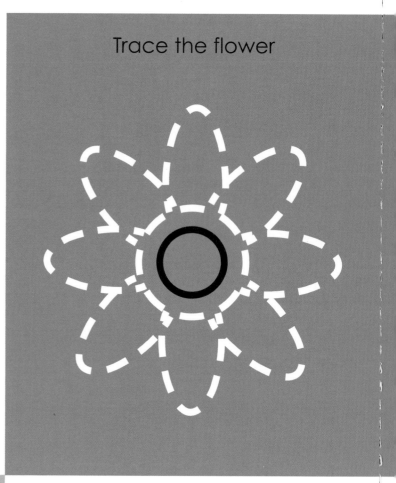

Look at the tree

Trace the tree

28

Toys

Look at the teddy bear

Trace the teddy bear

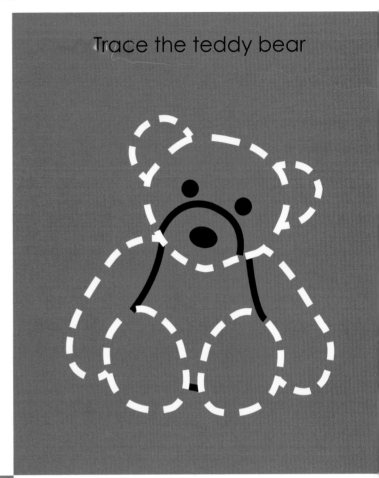

Look at the drum

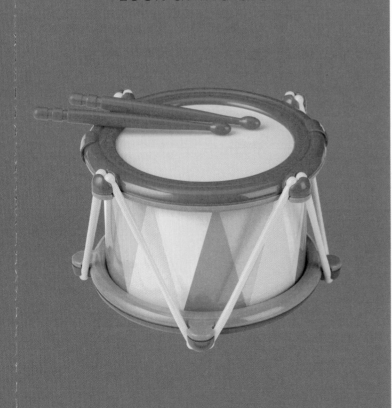

Trace the drum

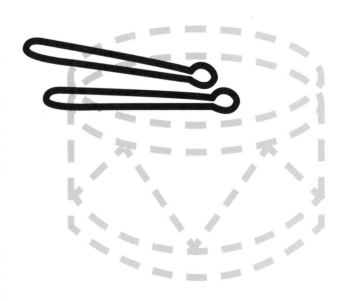

Let's Write ABC

Get ready to learn your letters!

 **a**nt

 a

 **a**pple

look at the letter

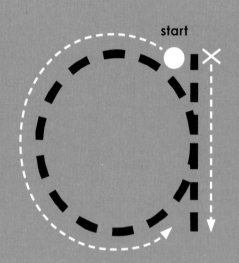
start

trace the letter

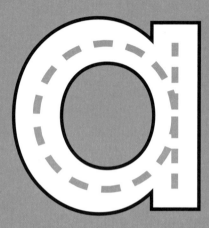
draw inside

Practice writing the letter a.

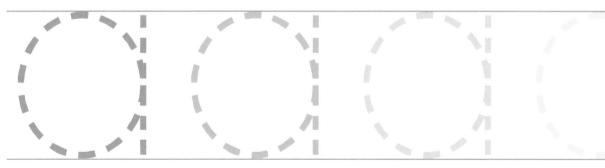

Now write it yourself.

 **A**corns

 A

look at the letter

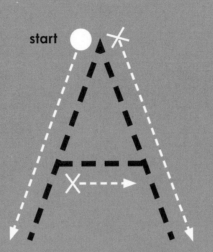

start

trace the letter

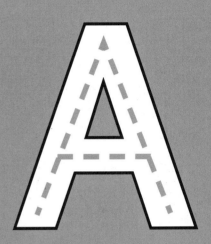

draw inside

Practice writing the letter A.

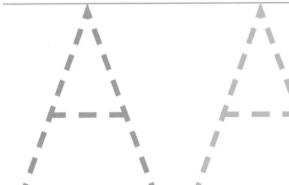

Now write it yourself.

bee

ball

look at the letter

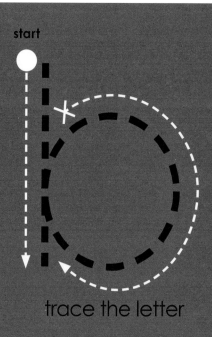
start

trace the letter

draw inside

Practice writing the letter b.

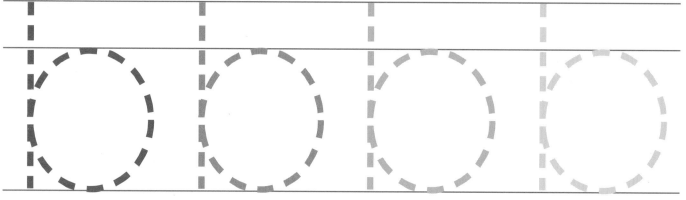

Now write it yourself.

  B is for butterfly!

B

Boat

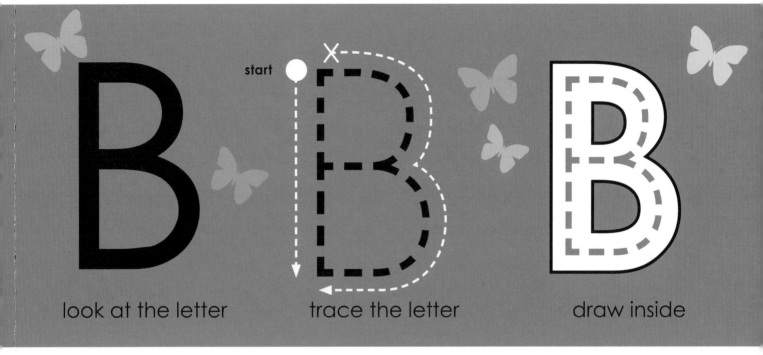

look at the letter   start   ✕   trace the letter   draw inside

Practice writing the letter B.

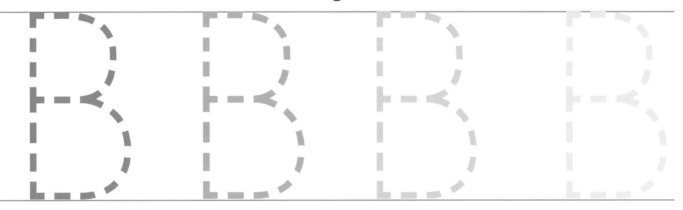

Now write it yourself.

What else can you think of that begins with "c"?

C

cupcake

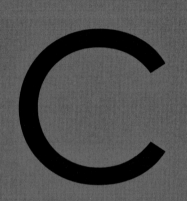

look at the letter

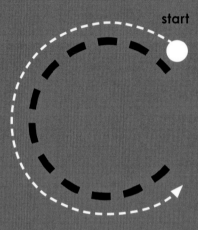

start

trace the letter

draw inside

Practice writing the letter c.

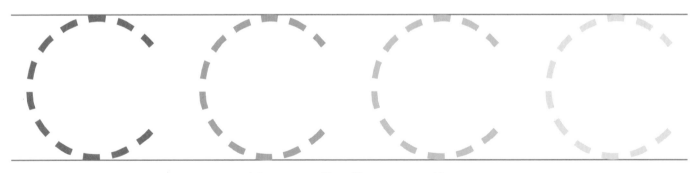

Now write it yourself.

 **C**at

 **C**

 **C**ar

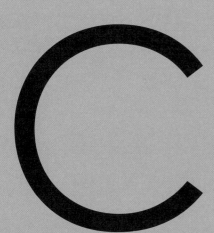 look at the letter

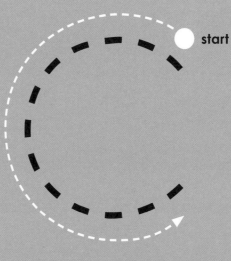 start

trace the letter

 draw inside

Practice writing the letter C.

Now write it yourself.

drum

D
is for
daisy!

look at the letter

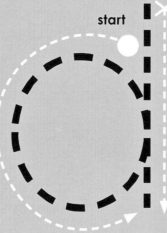

start

trace the letter

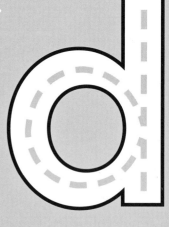

draw inside

Practice writing the letter d.

Now write it yourself.

 **D**oll

 D

 **D**uck

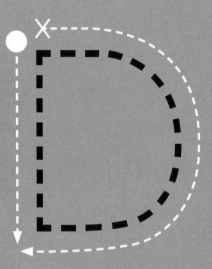

start

look at the letter

trace the letter

draw inside

Practice writing the letter D.

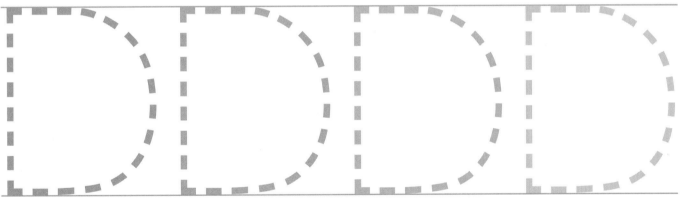

Now write it yourself.

 To trace an "e" start at the dot then follow it around.

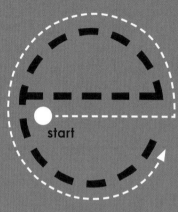 e

eagle

look at the letter

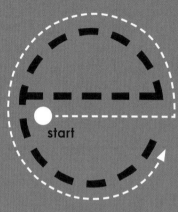

start

trace the letter

draw inside

Practice writing the letter e.

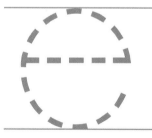 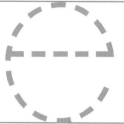

Now write it yourself.

 **E**gg

 E

 **E**lephant

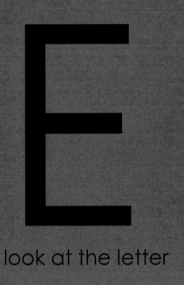 look at the letter

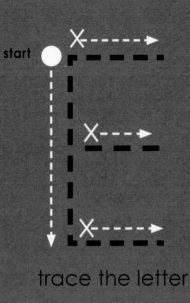 start

trace the letter

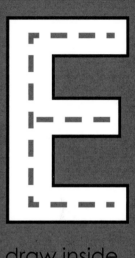 draw inside

Practice writing the letter E.

Now write it yourself.

 F is for FREEZING!

flower

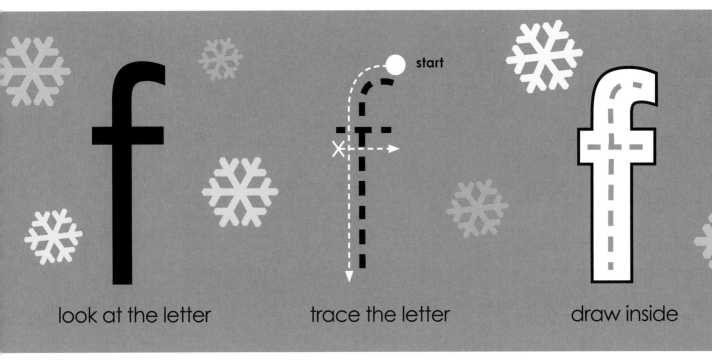

look at the letter

trace the letter   start

draw inside

Practice writing the letter f.

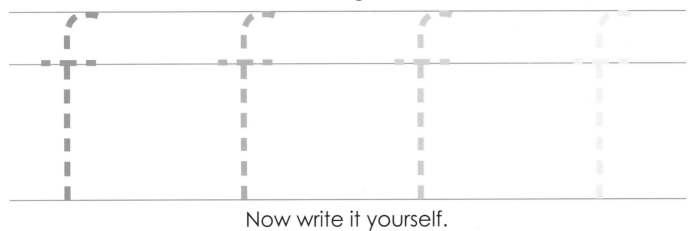

Now write it yourself.

Fish

F

Frog

look at the letter

trace the letter

draw inside

Practice writing the letter F.

Now write it yourself.

 **g**oat

 g

 **g**rapes

look at the letter

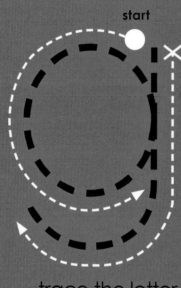
trace the letter

draw inside

Practice writing the letter g.

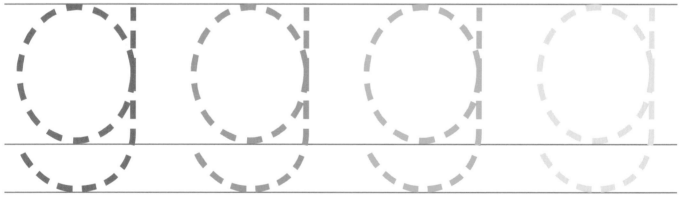

Now write it yourself.

 **G**

Gloves

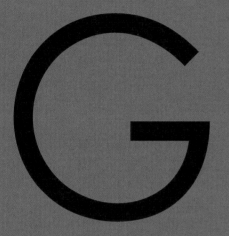

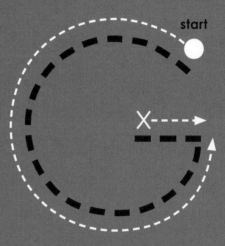

look at the letter

trace the letter

draw inside

What else can you think of that begins with "G"?

start

Practice writing the letter G.

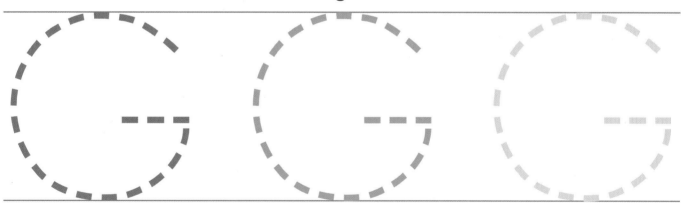

Now write it yourself.

hat

h

H is for hill!

start

look at the letter

trace the letter

draw inside

Practice writing the letter h.

Now write it yourself.

 **H**ouse

 H

 **H**en

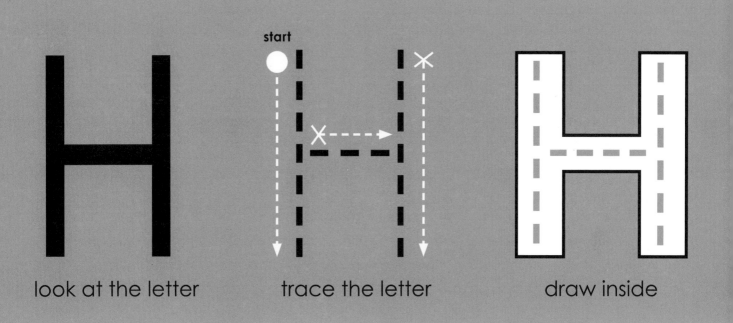

look at the letter   trace the letter   draw inside

Practice writing the letter H.

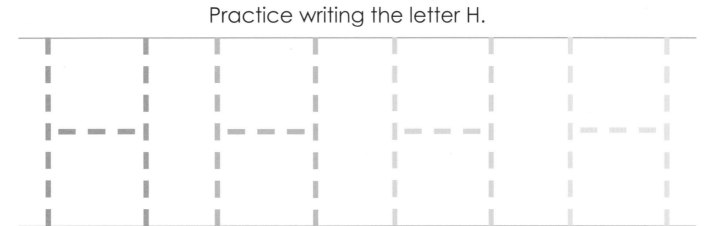

Now write it yourself.

What's your favorite ice cream?

i

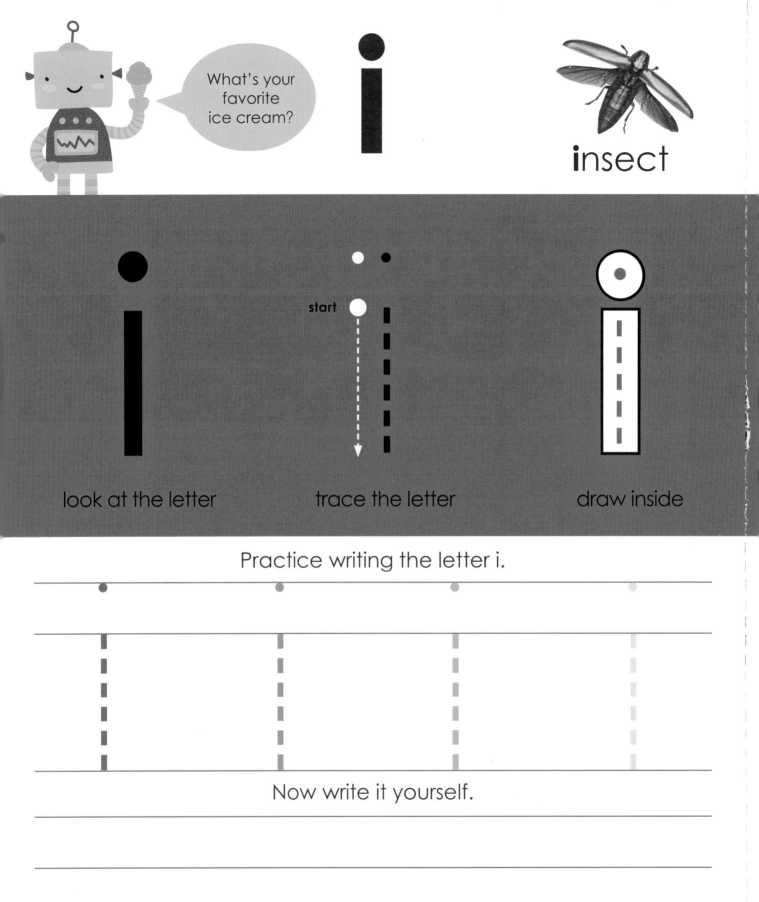

insect

look at the letter

start

trace the letter

draw inside

Practice writing the letter i.

Now write it yourself.

 **I**nk

 **I**ce cream

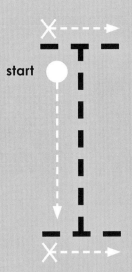

look at the letter

start

trace the letter

draw inside

Practice writing the letter I.

Now write it yourself.

J is for jellyfish!

j

jug

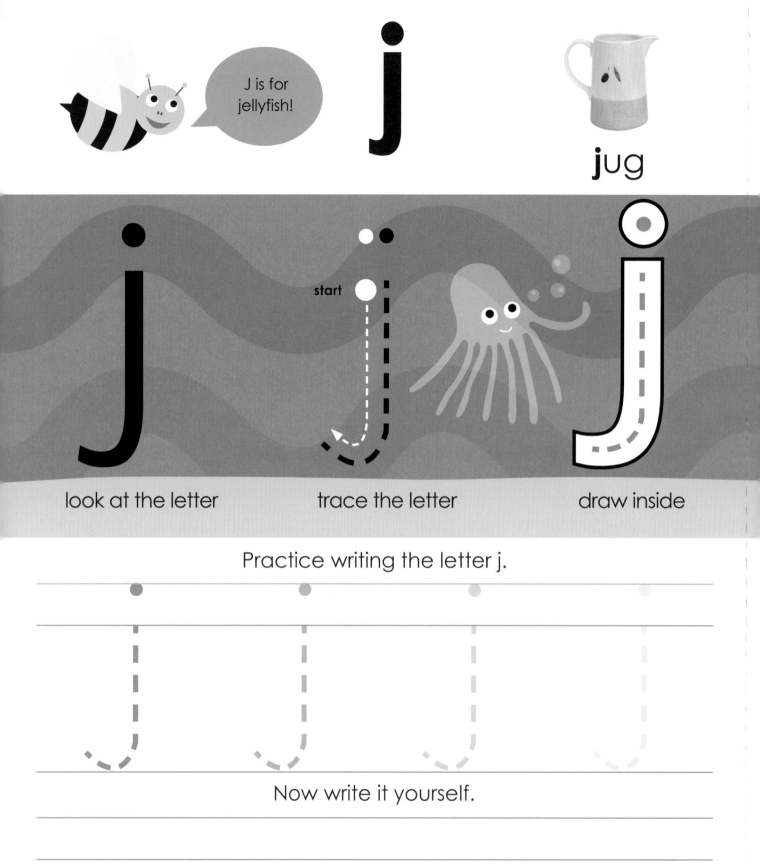

look at the letter

start

trace the letter

draw inside

Practice writing the letter j.

Now write it yourself.

 **J**uice

 J

 **J**elly

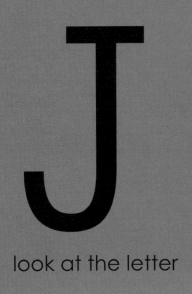

look at the letter

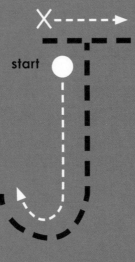

start

trace the letter

draw inside

Practice writing the letter J.

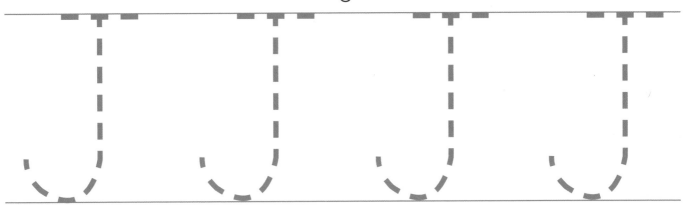

Now write it yourself.

kiwifruit

Keep practicing!

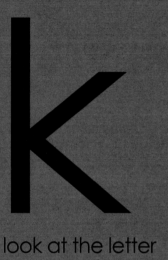

look at the letter

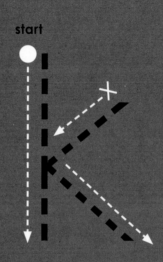

start

trace the letter

draw inside

Practice writing the letter k.

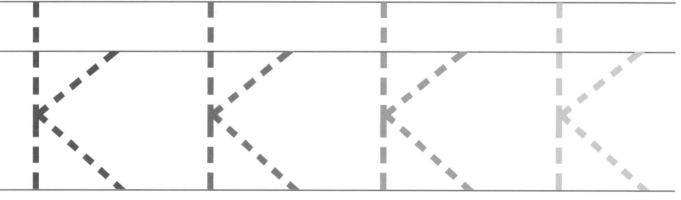

Now write it yourself.

Kite

Kitten

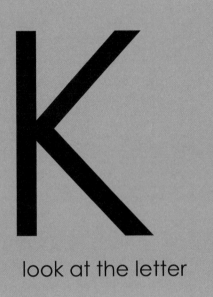

look at the letter

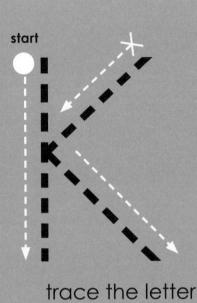

start

trace the letter

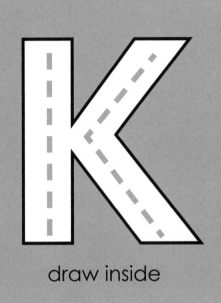

draw inside

Practice writing the letter K.

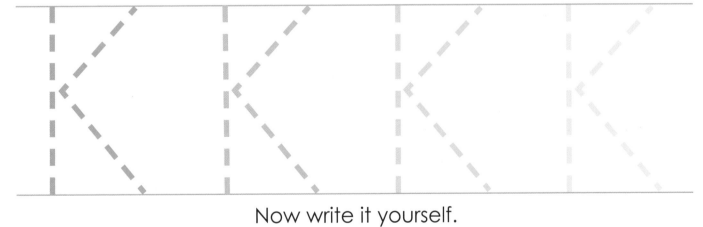

Now write it yourself.

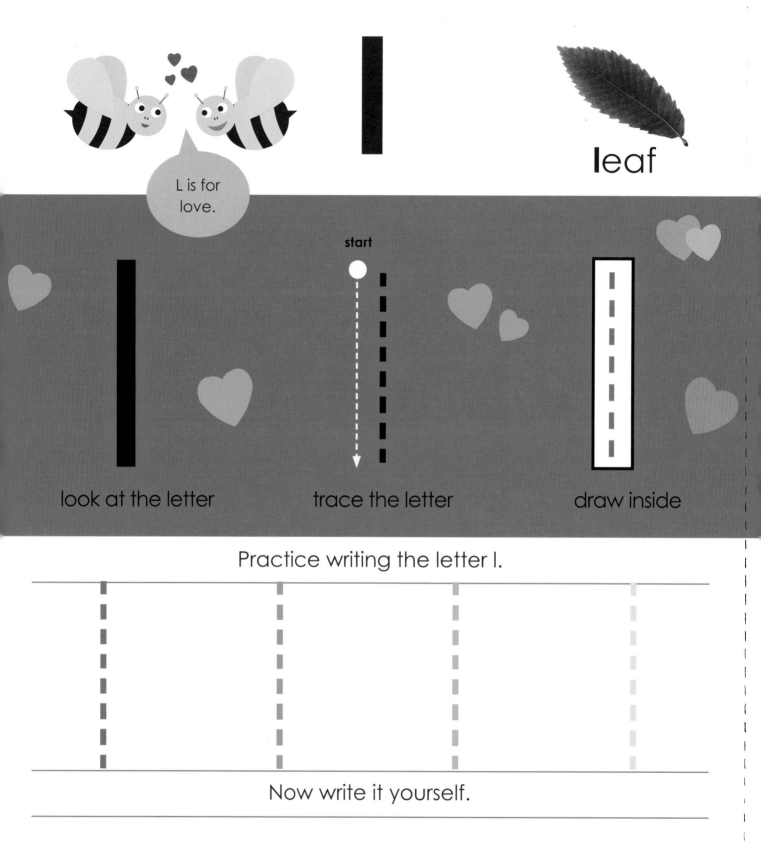

L is for love.

leaf

start

look at the letter

trace the letter

draw inside

Practice writing the letter l.

Now write it yourself.

Lion

L

Lemon

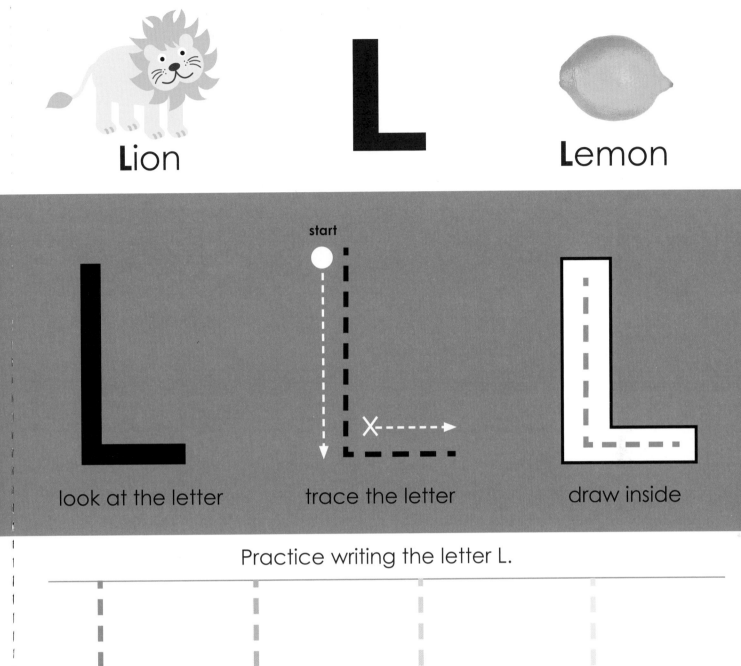

look at the letter

start

trace the letter

draw inside

Practice writing the letter L.

Now write it yourself.

mouse

milk

look at the letter   trace the letter   draw inside

Practice writing the letter m.

Now write it yourself.

Keep going. You are doing really well!

M

Moon

start

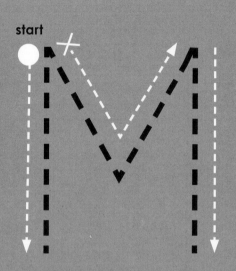

look at the letter

trace the letter

draw inside

Practice writing the letter M.

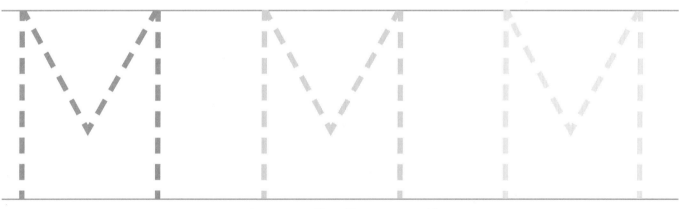

Now write it yourself.

nut

n

nest

look at the letter

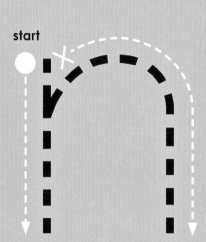
start

trace the letter

draw inside

Practice writing the letter n.

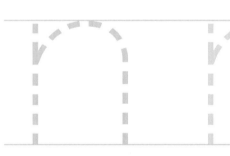

Now write it yourself.

Net

N

N is for night.

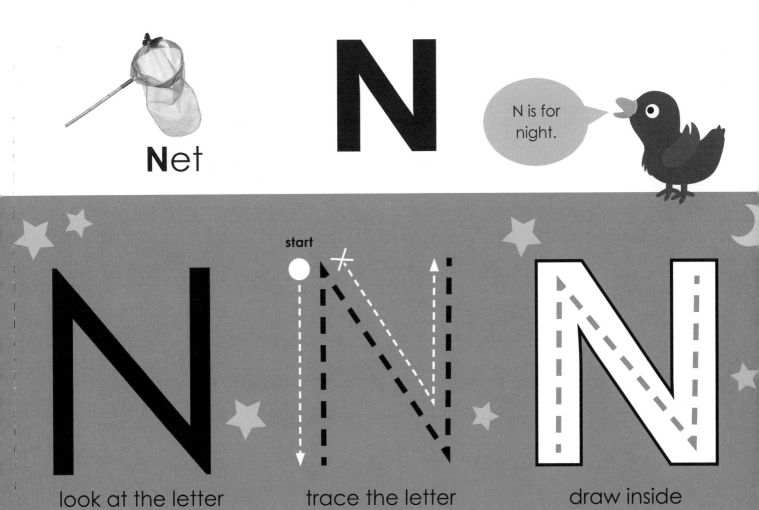

look at the letter

start

trace the letter

draw inside

Practice writing the letter N.

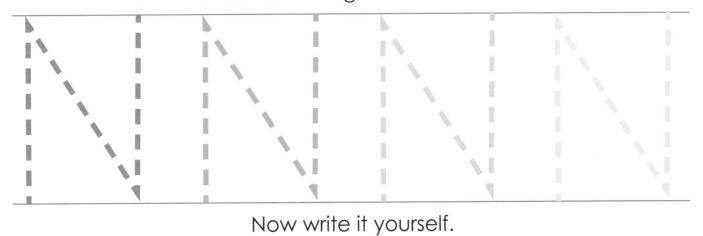

Now write it yourself.

orange

What shape is an orange?

look at the letter

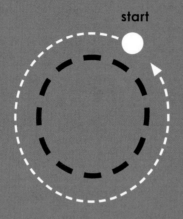

start

trace the letter

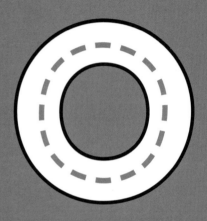

draw inside

Practice writing the letter o.

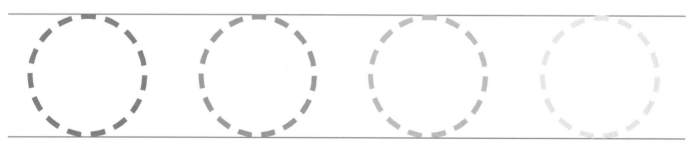

Now write it yourself.

60

Owl

Octopus

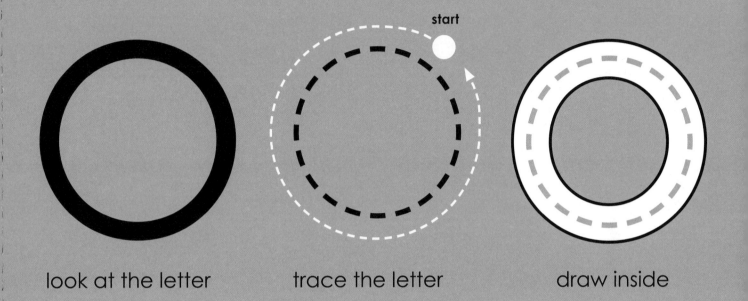

look at the letter   trace the letter   draw inside

Practice writing the letter O.

Now write it yourself.

What says "Oink, oink"?

p

pear

look at the letter

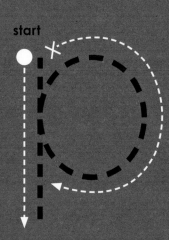

start

trace the letter

draw inside

Practice writing the letter p.

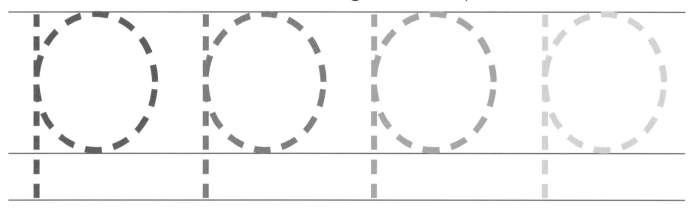

Now write it yourself.

 **P**aints

 P

 **P**ig

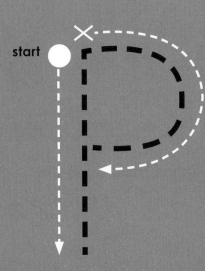

look at the letter

trace the letter   start ✕

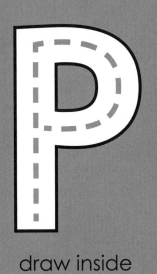

draw inside

Practice writing the letter P.

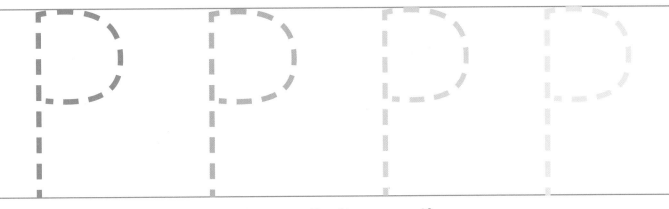

Now write it yourself.

queen

quiet

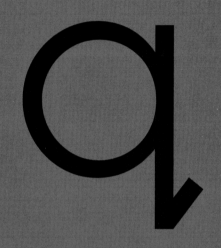
look at the letter

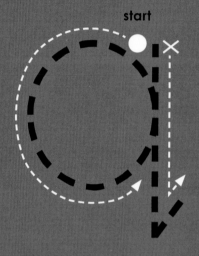
start
trace the letter

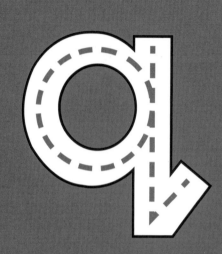
draw inside

Practice writing the letter q.

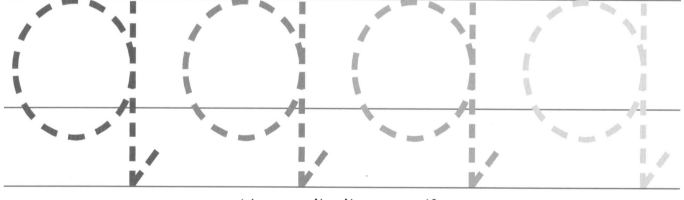

Now write it yourself.

What "q" is wearing a crown?

Q

Quilt

look at the letter

trace the letter

start

draw inside

Practice writing the letter Q.

Now write it yourself.

 **r**obot

 **r**

 **r**abbit

look at the letter

start

trace the letter

draw inside

Practice writing the letter r.

Now write it yourself.

66

Ring

 R

R is for rose.

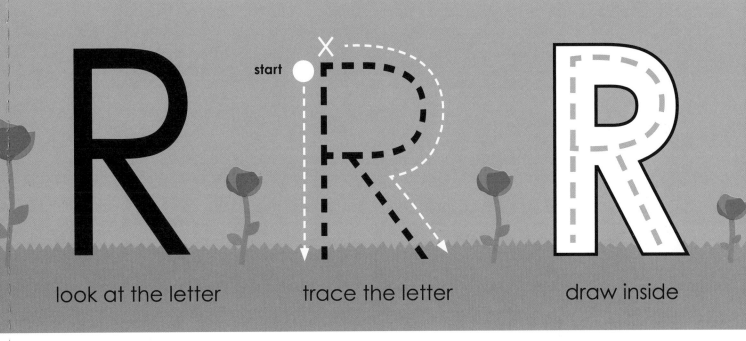

look at the letter   trace the letter   draw inside

Practice writing the letter R.

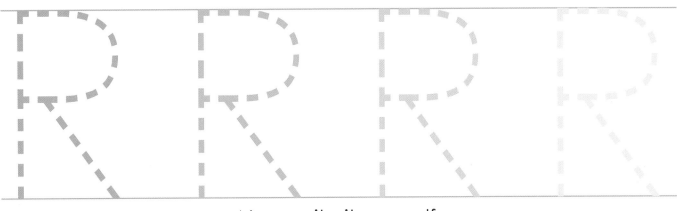

Now write it yourself.

shoes

Can you think of anything else that begins with "s"?

look at the letter

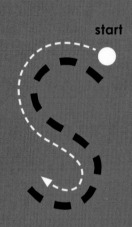

start

trace the letter

draw inside

Practice writing the letter s.

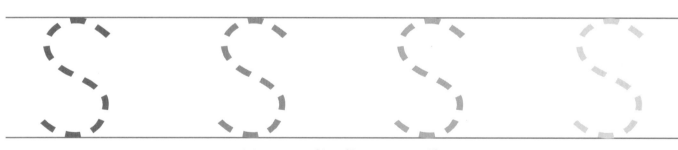

Now write it yourself.

Sheep

Snake

look at the letter

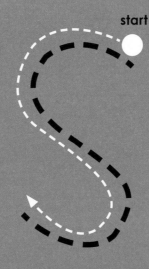

start

trace the letter

draw inside

Practice writing the letter S.

Now write it yourself.

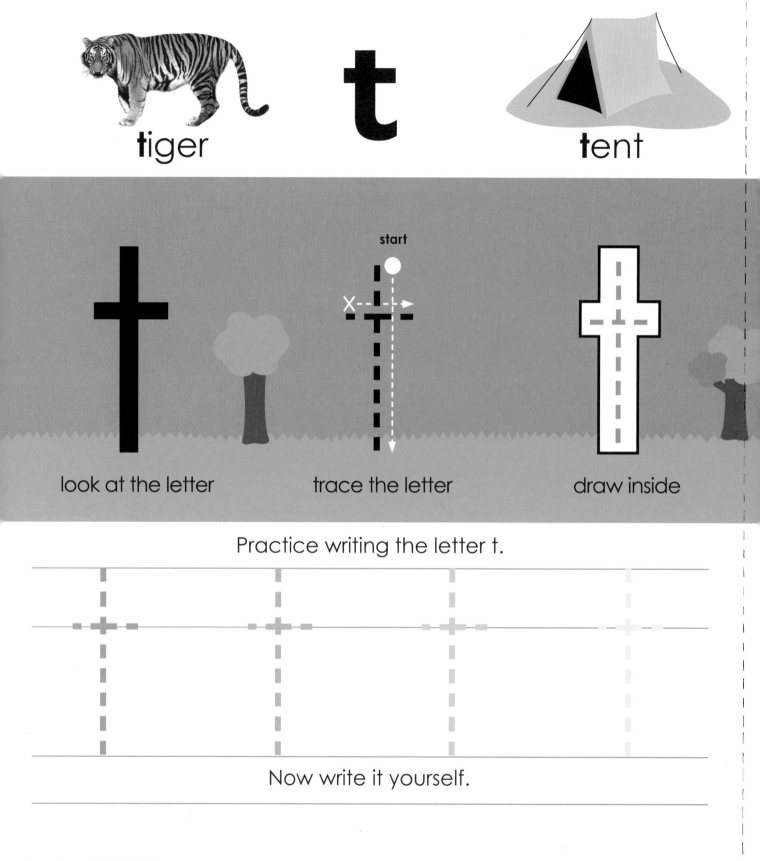

t

tiger

tent

look at the letter

start

trace the letter

draw inside

Practice writing the letter t.

Now write it yourself.

70

T

T is for tree.

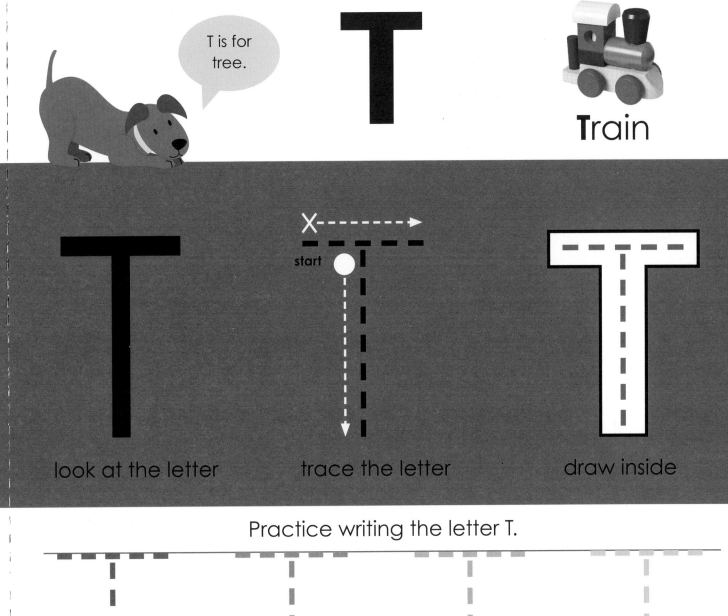

Train

look at the letter

start

trace the letter

draw inside

Practice writing the letter T.

Now write it yourself.

Well done. You have almost completed this section!

U

undress

look at the letter

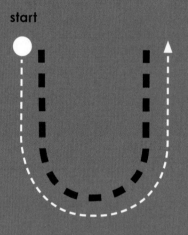

start

trace the letter

draw inside

Practice writing the letter u.

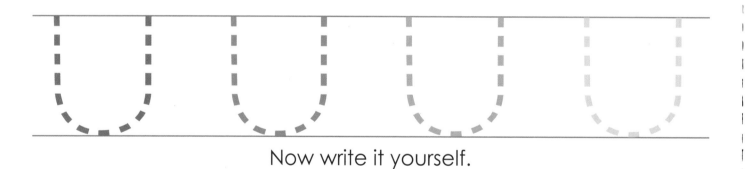

Now write it yourself.

 **U**mbrella

 U

 **U**p

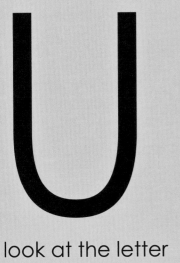

look at the letter

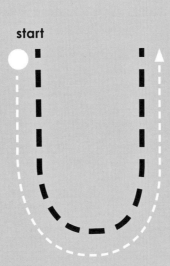

start

trace the letter

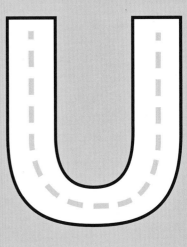

draw inside

Practice writing the letter U.

Now write it yourself.

vase

Do you know any other words that begin with "v"?

look at the letter

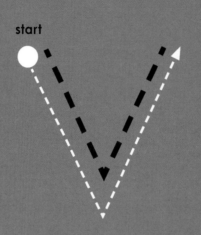

start

trace the letter

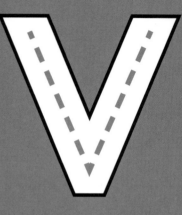

draw inside

Practice writing the letter v.

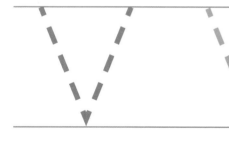

Now write it yourself.

Van

Vegetables

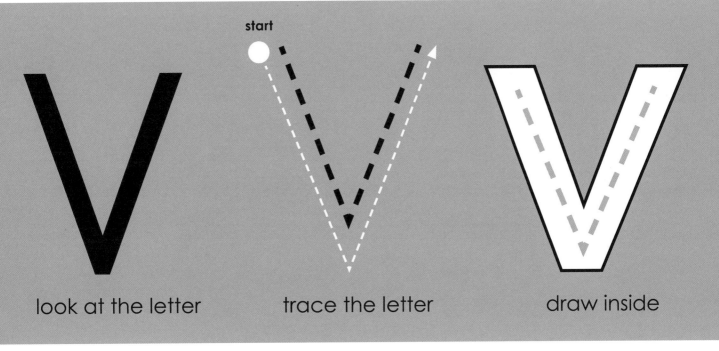

look at the letter

trace the letter

draw inside

Practice writing the letter V.

Now write it yourself.

W is for waves.

W

whale

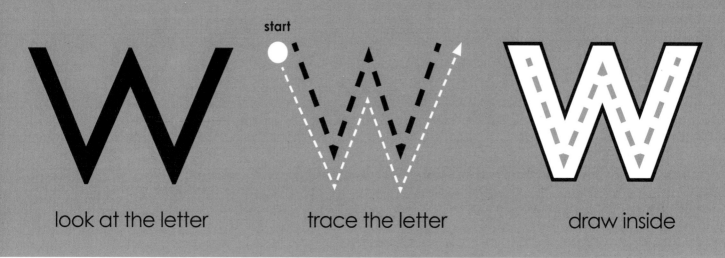

look at the letter

start

trace the letter

draw inside

Practice writing the letter w.

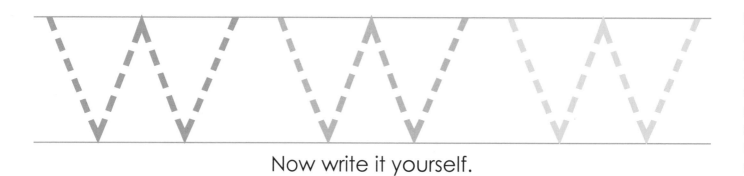

Now write it yourself.

Wheel

W

Watch

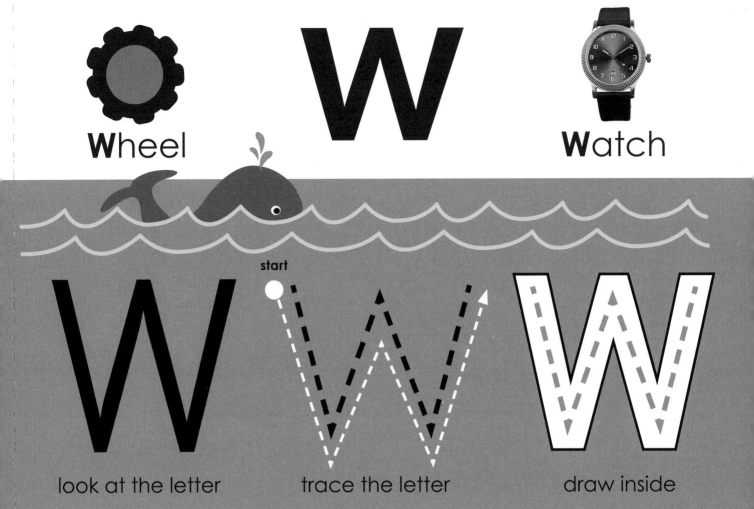

look at the letter   trace the letter   draw inside

start

Practice writing the letter W.

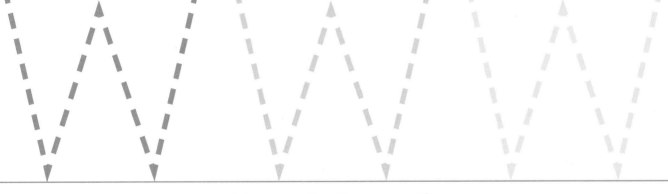

Now write it yourself.

xylophone

x

bo**x**

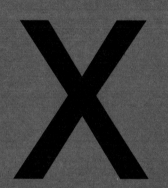

look at the letter

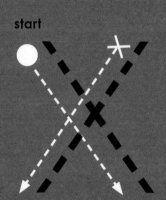

start

trace the letter

draw inside

Practice writing the letter x.

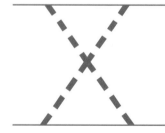

Now write it yourself.

78

What is the X-ray of?

X

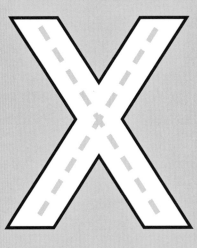

X-ray

look at the letter

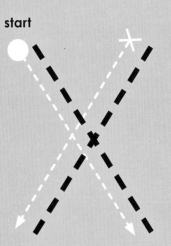

start

trace the letter

X

draw inside

Practice writing the letter X.

Now write it yourself.

yo-**y**o

What color begins with a "y"?

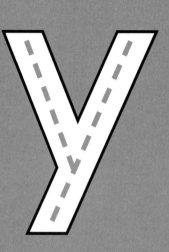

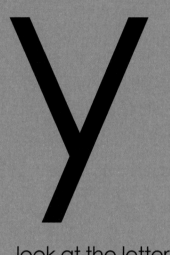

look at the letter

start

trace the letter

draw inside

Practice writing the letter y.

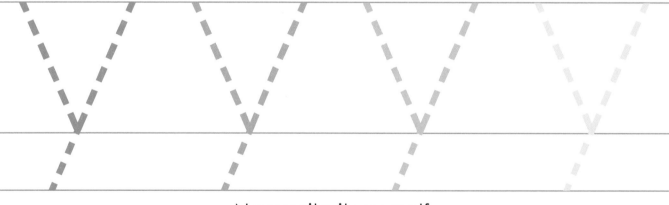

Now write it yourself.

 **Y**acht

 Y

 **Y**ogurt

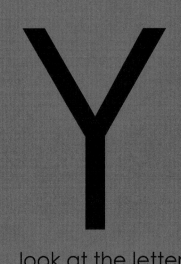

look at the letter

start

trace the letter

draw inside

Practice writing the letter Y.

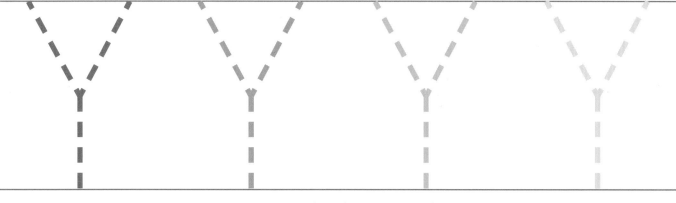

Now write it yourself.

zoo

z

zipper

Z

look at the letter

start

Z

trace the letter

Z

draw inside

Practice writing the letter z.

Now write it yourself.

82

Zebra

You are a superstar!

look at the letter

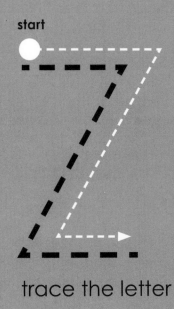

start

trace the letter

draw inside

Practice writing the letter Z.

Now write it yourself.

Lowercase alphabet

Trace over each letter of the lowercase alphabet.

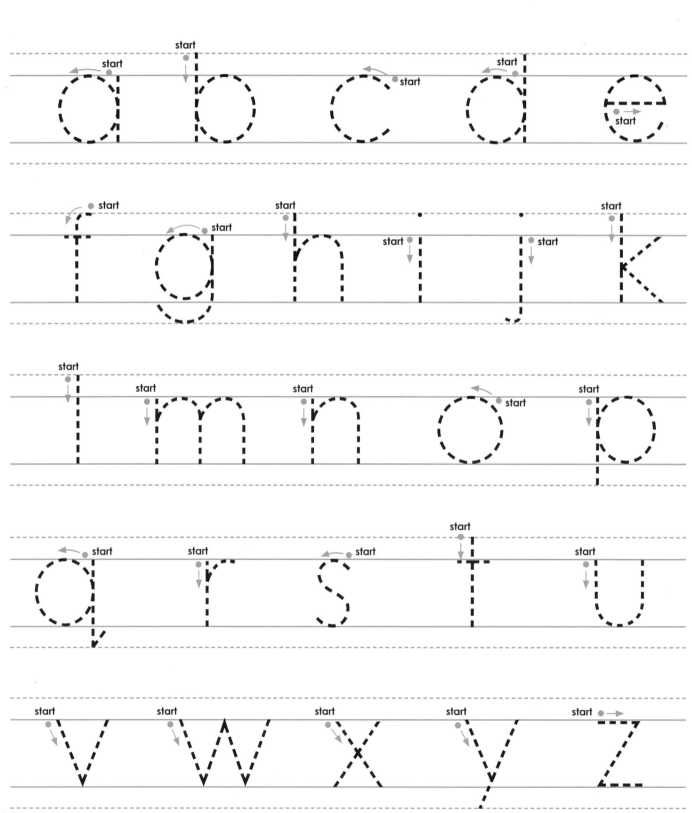

Uppercase alphabet

Trace over each letter of the uppercase alphabet.

Grid search

Circle all the lowercase letters in the grid.

h	R	a	F	D	J
G	d	A	f	E	V
y	H	n	K	Z	L
N	S	T	m	O	Q
g	W	C	I	B	P
M	e	t	U	X	Y

Can you find the first letter of your name in the grid?

What's missing?

Fill in the missing letters to complete the lowercase alphabet.

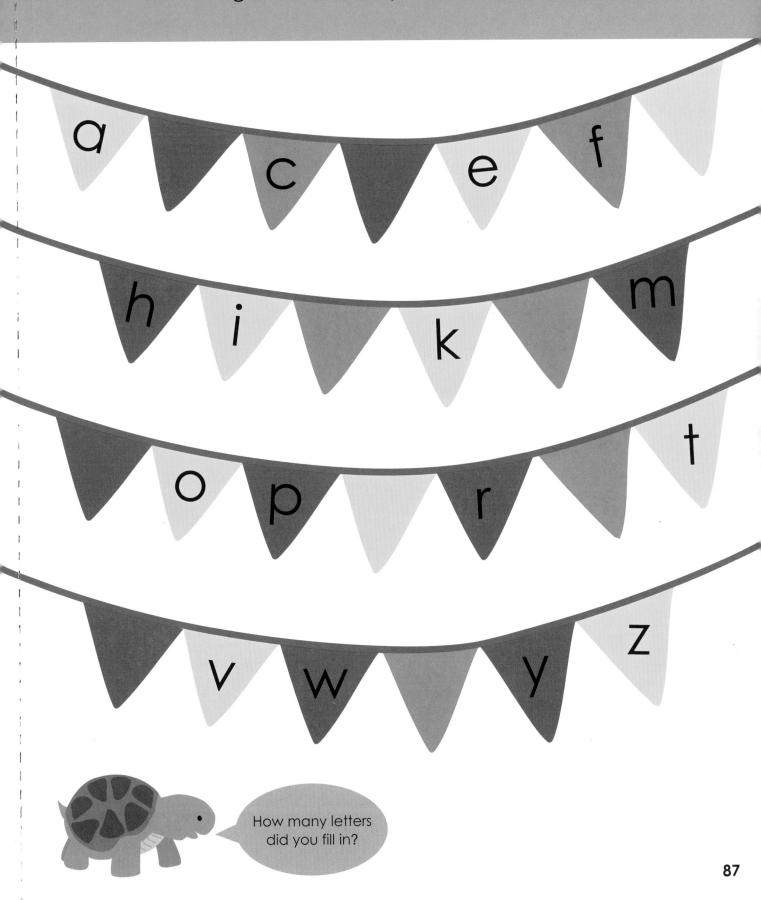

a c e f

h i k m

o p r t

v w y z

How many letters
did you fill in?

Grid search

Circle all the uppercase letters in the grid.

Y	r	A	f	d	j
g	D	a	F	E	U
Y	h	n	K	Z	L
N	s	t	m	o	Q
G	B	c	i	b	P
e	T	U	X	Y

How many **Y**s did you find?

What's missing?

Fill in the missing letters to complete the uppercase alphabet.

A C E F

H I K M

O P R T

V W Y Z

How many missing letters have you written?

Sight Words

Some words are trickier to say and spell than others.

The word "a" can make two sounds—a long "ay", as in "day", or a short "a", as in "apple".

say the word

draw inside

trace the word

now write the word

The word "a" is used when writing about a thing or a person.
Write "a" in these two sentences.

I am _____ mouse.
I have _____ brother.

 # an

The "a" in "an" is a short "a" sound, as in "ant".

say the word

draw inside

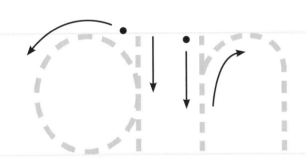

trace the word

now write the word

You use "an" before a word that begins with a **vowel** (a, e, i, o, u). Write the word in these sentences.

I am _____ orange fox.

You are _____ elephant.

You use "am" a lot when writing about yourself: "I am a cat".

am

I am a child!

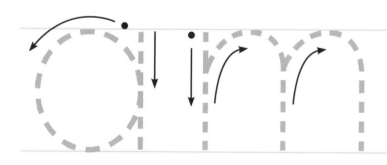

say the word

draw inside

trace the word

now write the word

The words "am" and "an" look similar but are used in different ways. Write them in this sentence.

I _____ eating
ice cream cone.

and

Learning the word "and" by sight will really help your reading.

and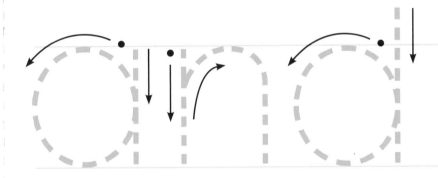

say the word

draw inside

trace the word

now write the word

In a sentence, "and" is a joining word. Write it in this sentence.

Mary _____ Mia are hugging.

are

In the word "are" the "e" on the end is silent. You just say the "ar" sound like in "car".

are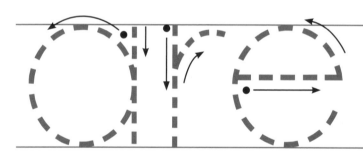

say the word

draw inside

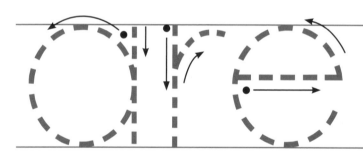

trace the word

now write the word

Circle the word "are" when it appears in the sentence.

The children are having a party.

I

Don't be tricked by the word "I". It makes a long "y" sound like in "fly".

say the word

draw inside

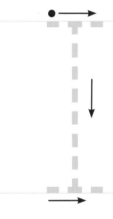

trace the word

now write the word

Circle the words that rhyme with "I".

fly	sky	my
can	hen	pin
try	shy	mat

me

say the word

draw inside

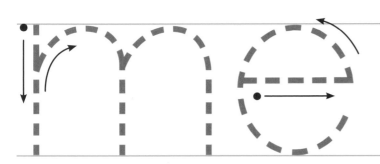

trace the word

now write the word

Circle the word shape that matches **me**

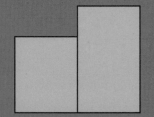

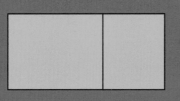

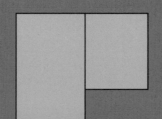

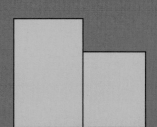

my

In "my", the letter "y" makes a long "y" sound, as in "sky".

my my

say the word   draw inside

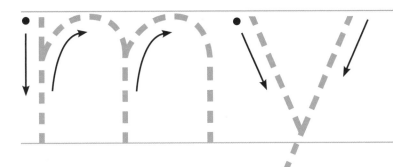

trace the word   now write the word

Can you fill in the missing word in the sentence?

This is _____ bike.

99

he

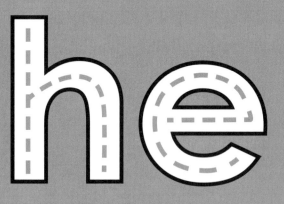

In "he", the letter "e" makes a long "ee" sound, like in "tree".

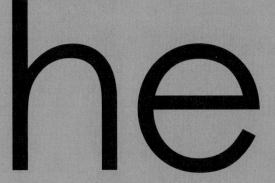

say the word

he

draw inside

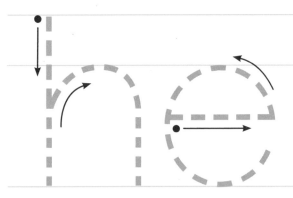

trace the word

now write the word

Can you write in the missing word in this sentence?

I like Thomas; _____
_____ is my friend.

she

In "she", the "e" makes a long "ee" sound, like in "bee".

she she

say the word

draw inside

trace the word

now write the word

Circle the words that rhyme with "she".

| me | sky | tree | got |
| pan | sit | he | tap |

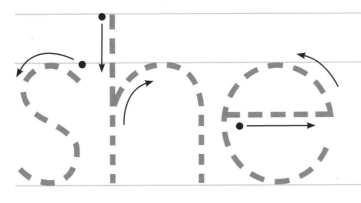

the

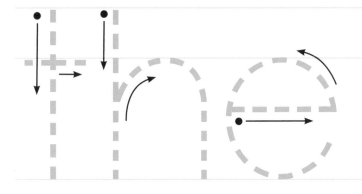

say the word

the

draw inside

trace the word

now write the word

Circle the word "the" when it appears in the sentence.

The dog runs

after the ball.

they

In "they", the letters "ey" together make a long "ay" sound, like in "hay".

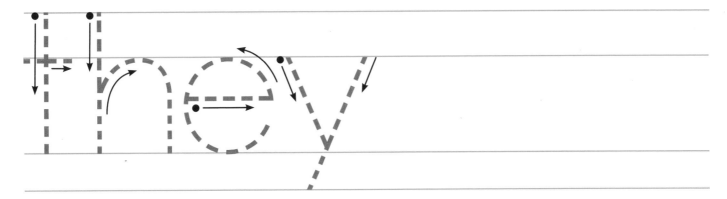

say the word

draw inside

trace the word

now write the word

Trace the sentence below that uses the word "they".

They like to bake cakes.

The "s" in "is" sounds like the "z" in "zebra".

is

is

say the word

is

draw inside

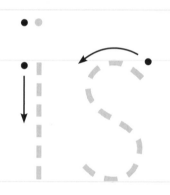

trace the word

now write the word

The word "is" is used a lot. Write it in these sentences.

This _____ my house.

When _____ your birthday?

this

The "s" in "this" sounds like the "s" in "snake".

this

say the word

draw inside

trace the word

now write the word

Change the word "ship" to the word "this" by changing one letter at a time.

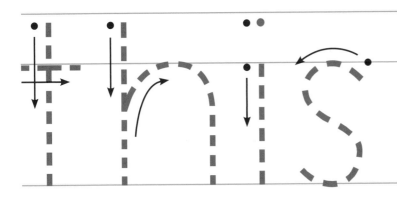

ship → chip → chin → thin → this

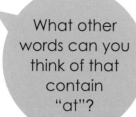

What other words can you think of that contain "at"?

at

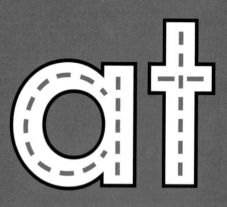

say the word

draw inside

trace the word

now write the word

When you read, you will see words written in different ways.
Which of these **does not** say "at"?

At   at   at   et   AT   at

up

up

say the word

up

draw inside

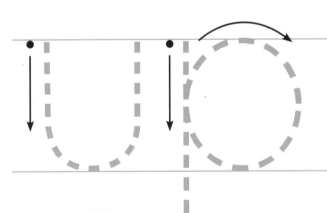

trace the word

now write the word

Circle the word "up" in the sentence below.

The balloons fly up in the air.

  **SO**

In the word "so", the letter "o" makes a long "oh" sound, as in "slow".

SO

say the word

draw inside

trace the word

now write the word

Circle the word that **doesn't** rhyme with "so".

no	show	mow	he
slow	low	tow	toe

108

go

go

say the word

go

draw inside

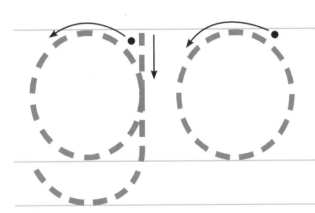

trace the word

now write the word

Trace the sentence below that uses the word "go".

I would like to
go swimming.

109

When you write the letter "i" you need to lift your pen to make the dot.

 say the word

 draw inside

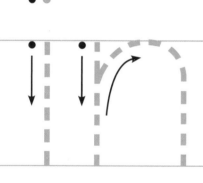 trace the word

now write the word

Trace the sentence below that uses the word "in".

The spider is
in the web.

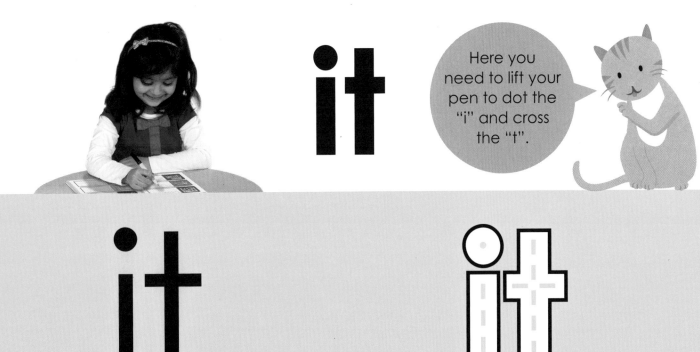

it

Here you need to lift your pen to dot the "i" and cross the "t".

say the word

draw inside

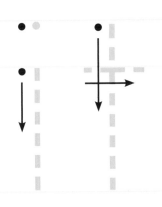

trace the word

now write the word

Words are valuable, like treasure! Find the real words and draw lines to the treasure chest.

bit

wut

fit

mep

sit

ib

lom

it

do

Don't be tricked by the letter "o" here. It makes an "ou" sound, as in "boo".

do

say the word

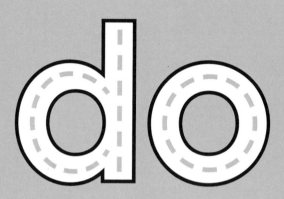

draw inside

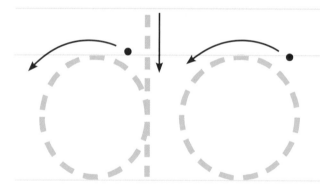

trace the word

now write the word

Trace the sentence below that uses the word "do".

When do you get up?

 Boo!

to

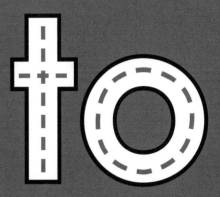 "To" is like "do" but with a "t" instead of a "d".

to

say the word

to

draw inside

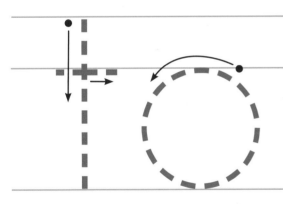

trace the word

now write the word

Can you write in the missing word in this sentence?

We are going _____ school.

In the word "on", the letter "o" makes a short "o" sound, as in "octopus".

 on

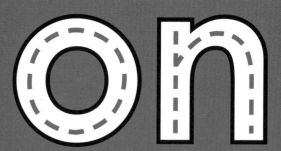

say the word

draw inside

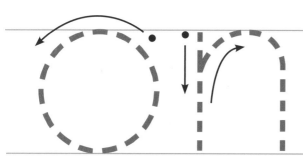

trace the word

now write the word

Circle the word "on" in the sentence below.

No one is sitting on the chair.

114

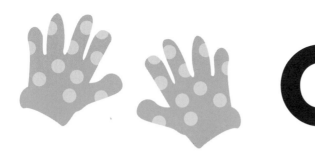

of

say the word

draw inside

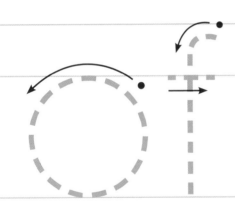

trace the word

now write the word

It is easy to confuse the words "of" and "off". Circle both in the sentence below and say them out loud when you do.

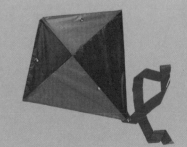

The tail of the kite flew off in the wind.

115

Can you see me?

we

In "we", the "e" makes a long "ee" sound, like in "see".

we we

say the word

draw inside

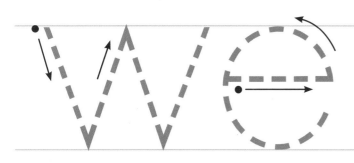

trace the word

now write the word

Trace the sentence below that uses the word "we".

We like to go to the beach.

you

In "you", the letters "ou" make a long "oo" sound, like in "moo".

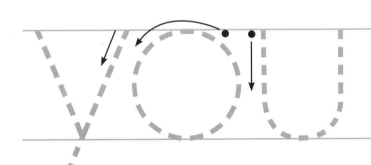

say the word

draw inside

trace the word

now write the word

Circle the words that rhyme with "you".

you

to	hi	zoo
rat	blue	pig
do	van	wet

can

If you can spell "an", then "can" is easy; just add the letter "c".

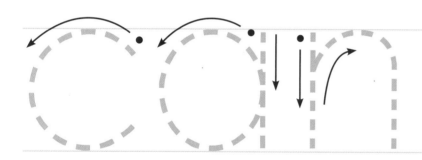

say the word   draw inside

trace the word   now write the word

The word "can" is both a **verb** and a **noun**. Finish these sentences.

I can play the violin.

I open the can.

day

day day

say the word   draw inside

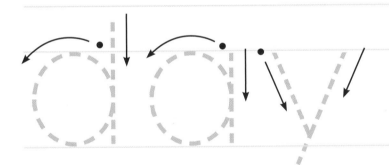

trace the word   now write the word

Circle the word "day" in each of these longer words.

Monday	Tuesday	Wednesday	Thursday
Friday	Saturday	Sunday	today

yes

The letter "y" is made with two strokes. You need to lift your pen.

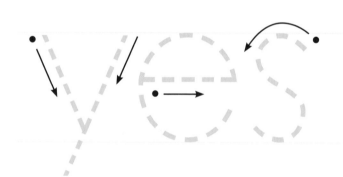

say the word

yes

draw inside

trace the word

now write the word

Write the word "yes" in this sentence.

I'd love pancakes,
_____, please!

In the word "no" the letter "o" makes a long "ow" sound, like in "snow".

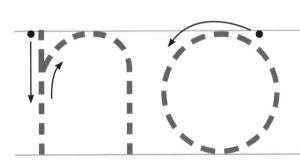

say the word

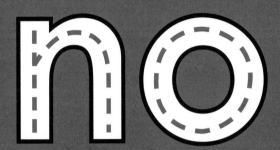

draw inside

trace the word

now write the word

Circle the word shape that matches

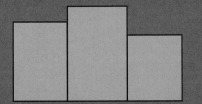 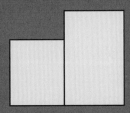 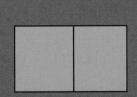 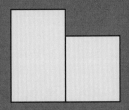

121

has

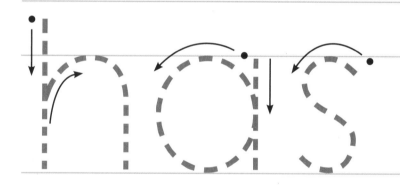

say the word

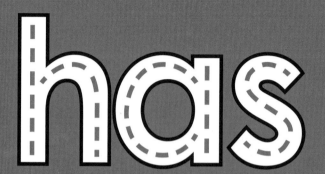

draw inside

trace the word

now write the word

Write the word "has" in this sentence.

The lamb ____

a wooly coat.

122

was

The word "was" is very tricky. Read the special tips below first.

was was

say the word

draw inside

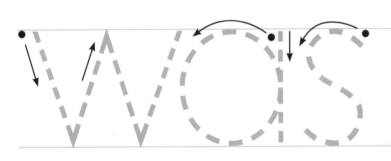

trace the word

now write the word

The letter "a" makes an "u" sound like in "duck".

The letter "s" makes a "z" sound like in "zoo."

be

In the word "be", the letter "e" makes a long "ee" sound, like in "sleep".

say the word

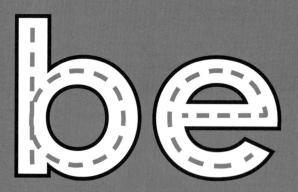

draw inside

trace the word

now write the word

Circle the word "be" when it appears in the sentence.

I want to be
a firefighter.

In the word "all", the letter "a" is making a sound, like "aw" in "paw".

say the word

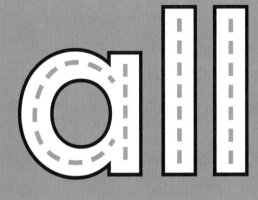

draw inside

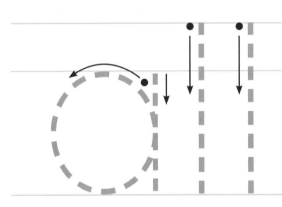

trace the word

now write the word

Circle the word shape that matches

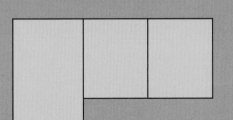

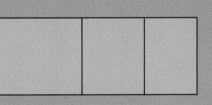

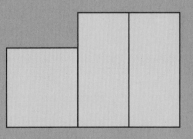

125

Shh, I am silent!

have

In the word "have" the letter "e" on the end is silent.

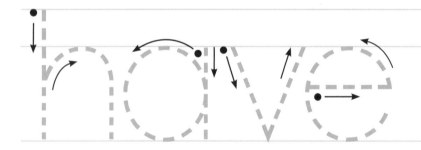

have have

say the word

draw inside

trace the word

now write the word

Circle the word "have" when it appears in the sentence.

I have lots of presents to open.

126

here

The word "here" is tricky. It sounds the same as "hear."

here   here

say the word   draw inside

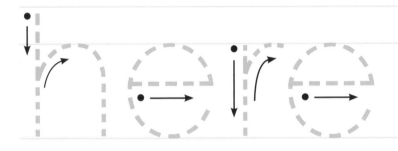

trace the word   now write the word

Circle the word that **doesn't** rhyme with "here".

hat   fear   hear

deer   year   ear

said

In "said", the letters "ai" make a short "e" sound like in "bed".

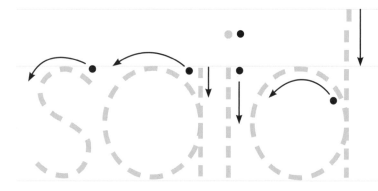

said said

say the word

draw inside

trace the word

now write the word

Trace the sentence below that uses the word "said".

"I love my teddy," said Louise.

see

The "ee" in "see" is a long sound. It rhymes with "bee" and "me".

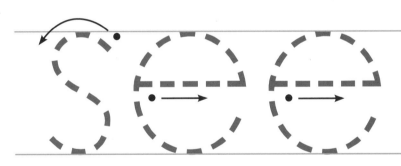

say the word

draw inside

trace the word

now write the word

Write the word "see" in this sentence.

I can _____ the stars.

him

In the word "him", the "im" makes the same sound as "swim".

him him

say the word   draw inside

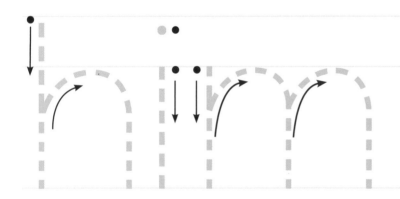

trace the word   now write the word

Circle the words that **don't** rhyme with "him".

| cat | swim | she | no |
| rim | yes | yet | dim |

her

In the word "her" the letters "er" make the "ur" sound, like in "fur".

her **her**

say the word   draw inside

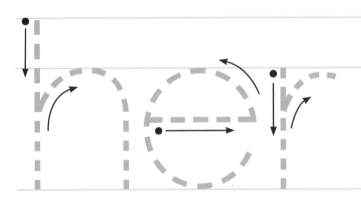

trace the word   now write the word

Circle the words that rhyme with "her".

stir	cap	him	fur
pat	blur	trap	met

into

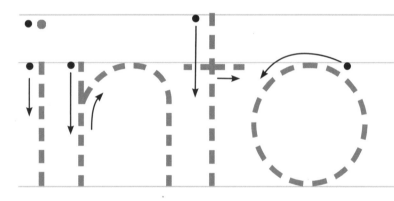

into into

say the word

draw inside

trace the word

now write the word

Circle the word "into" when it appears in the sentence.

The bat flew

into the cave.

like

like like

say the word

draw inside

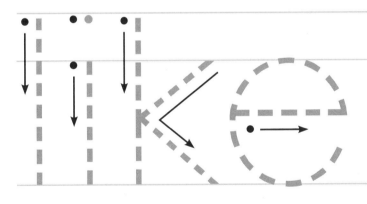

trace the word

now write the word

Fill in the missing "i" and "e" in these words. Then read them aloud.

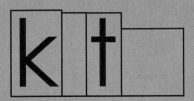 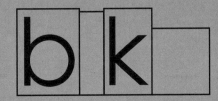 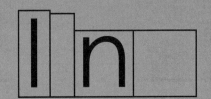

First Words

With 60 words to learn, trace, and write!

Animals

What sound does a dog make?

Animals

cat

cat

dog

dog

lion

tiger

bear

cow

cow

sheep

sheep

horse

horse

duck

duck

chick

chick

owl

owl

139

Food

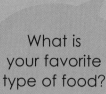
What is your favorite type of food?

Food

apple

apple

pear

pear

140

orange

grapes

cherry

egg

bread

peas

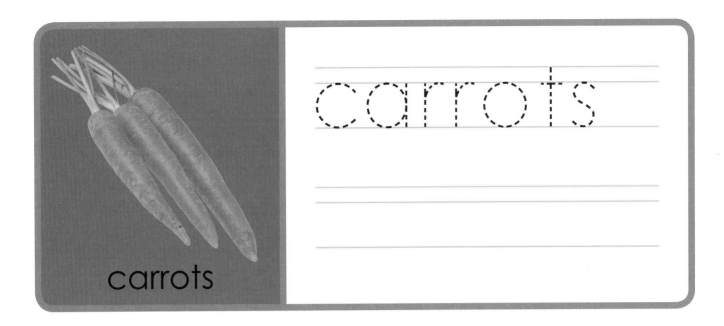

carrots

tomato

cheese

Clothes

Clothes

coat

coat

hat

hat

boots

b o o t s

socks

s o c k s

shoes

s h o e s

T-shirt

T-shirt

shorts

shorts

dress

dress

146

pants

p a n t s

shirt

shirt

skirt

skirt

Things that go

Which vehicles have you traveled in?

Things that go

car

car

truck

truck

148

bicycle

bicycle

plane

plane

bus

bus

tractor

tractor

digger

digger

taxi

taxi

train

train

tram

tram

boat

boat

Outside

What do you like to do outside?

Outside

tree

tree

flower

flower

leaf

sky

grass

stroller

stroller

ball

ball

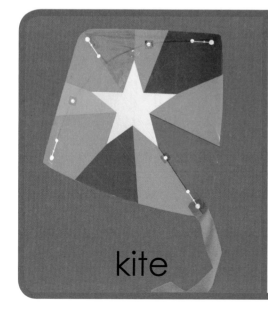

kite

kite

butterfly

butterfly

bee

bee

bird

bird

At home

Where do you like to read at home?

At home

table

table

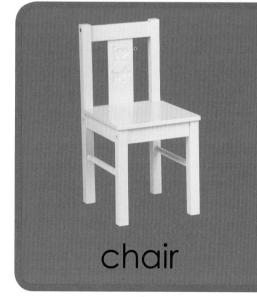

chair

chair

156

bed

b e d

toy

t o y

My big animal book

book

b o o k

knife

fork

spoon

plate

bowl

cup

Fun with Phonics

Learning phonics helps us to say, read, and write words!

Starting sounds

Trace each letter, then draw a line to connect the sound to the picture that begins with it.

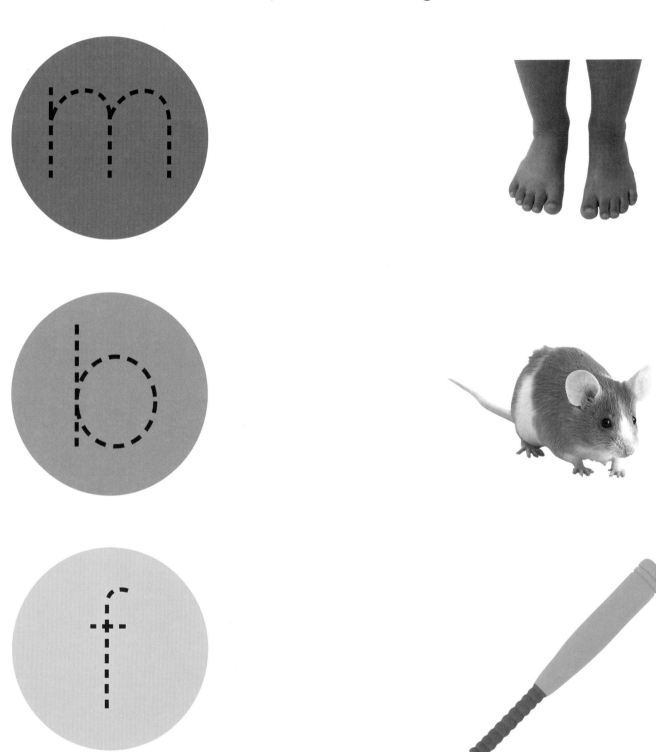

Starting sounds

Trace each letter, then draw a line to connect the
sound to the picture that begins with it.

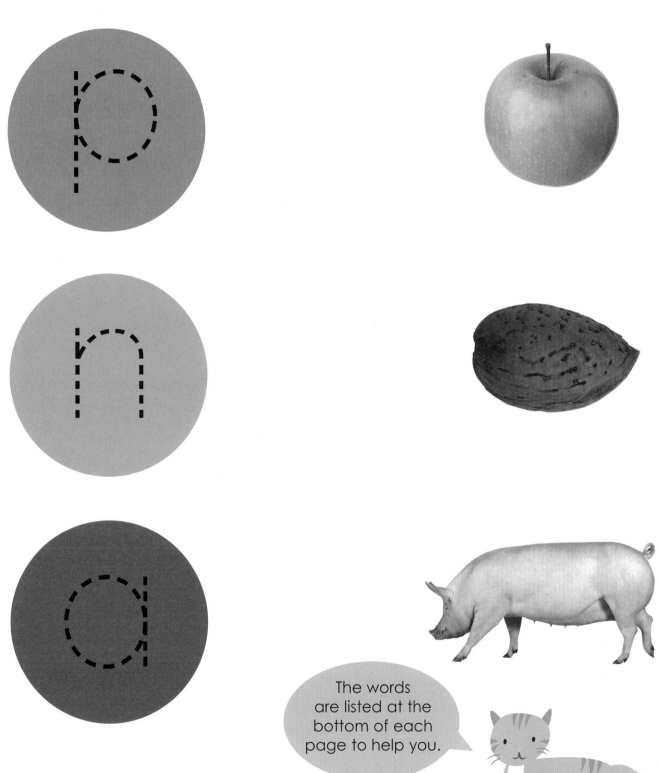

The words
are listed at the
bottom of each
page to help you.

Say the words: apple, nut, pig.

Matching sounds

Trace each letter, then connect the starting sound to the picture.

Say the words: ink, dog, tent.

Matching sounds

Trace each letter, then connect the starting sound to the picture.

What other words start with a "c"?

Say the words: cat, sun, jug.

Words and pictures

Draw a line between each picture and the
letter that makes its starting sound.

Which letter?

Look at each picture below, then circle the
letter that makes its starting sound.

Say the words: egg, milk, duck, cup.

Odd one out

Trace the letter at the beginning of each box, then cross out the picture that does not begin with the same sound.

Say the words: lamp, goat, lemon, dress, fan, fish.

Odd one out

Trace the letter at the beginning of each box, then cross out the picture that does not begin with the same sound.

Use the word list to help.

Say the words: hat, bag, hand, pig, pen, bed.

End sounds

Trace over the letter sound at the end of each word.

jug

up

milk

on

Say the words: jug, up, milk, on.

End sounds

Draw a line between each picture and the letter that makes its end sound.

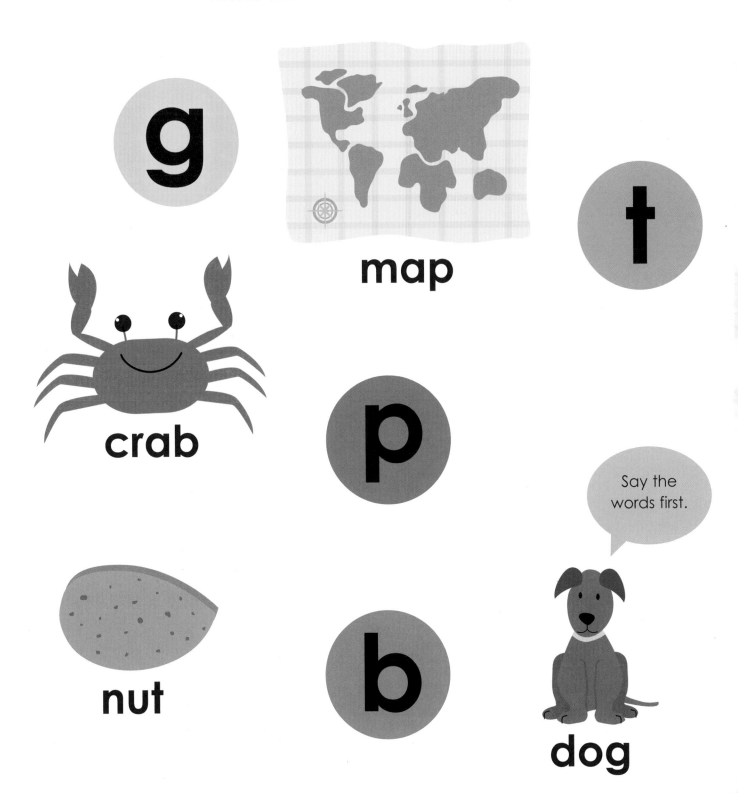

g

map

t

crab

p

Say the words first.

nut

b

dog

Sorting sounds

Check the box next to the word that matches
the picture in each section.

bug ☐ **bus** ☐

jet ☐ **jug** ☐

can ☐ **cup** ☐

log ☐ **rug** ☐

Say the words: bug, bus, jet, jug, can, cup, log, rug.

Sorting sounds

Trace over the last two letters in each word and then draw lines to connect the sound to the words with similar endings.

lap

ten

pen

hen

clap

These words also rhyme.

cap

Say the words: pen, hen, clap, cap.

Rhyming sounds

Trace over the last two letters in each word and say them out loud. Can you hear the rhyming sounds?

Why not make up a sentence that includes all these words?

cat   mat   hat

van   man   fan

Rhyming sounds

Draw lines to connect each end sound to
the word that rhymes with it.

ship

jar

car

hug

rug

Trace
the sounds
first!

lip

Say the words: ship, jar, car, hug, rug, lip.

End sounds

Fill in the missing end letters for each word.

pe___

cla___

su___

Say the words: pet, clap, sun.

End sounds

Fill in the missing end letters for each word.

jum............

Say each word aloud first.

ti............

ho............

Say the words: jump, tin, hot.

Middle sounds

Circle the pictures that have the same middle sound as the top letter.

Say the words: chick, zipper, duck, red, ten, drum.

Middle sounds

Trace over the middle letters in the words below, then circle the three words that have the same middle sound.

What is the middle sound?

sad bed hug

cup sit plum

Rhyming pairs

Trace the word, then draw a line from each word to the picture that it rhymes with.

Say each picture word first to help you.

Say the rhyming words: pen and hen, fox and box, rock and sock.

Rhyming pairs

Trace the word, then draw a line from each
word to the picture that it rhymes with.

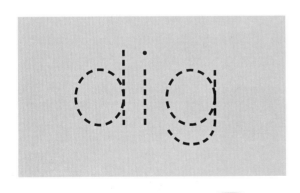

What else
rhymes with
"see"?

Say the words that rhyme: see and bee,
coat and goat, dig and pig.

Ch sounds

Trace over the letters, then draw lines
between the matching words and pictures.

Say the words: lunch, chick, catch, chest.

Sh sounds

Trace over the letters, then draw lines
between the matching words and pictures.

shell

shed

fish

ship

Do you know
any other words
that start with a
"sh" sound?

Say the words: ship, fish, shell, shed.

Oa sounds

Look at the sound in the red box. Trace the sound, then find it in the words below by underlining it.

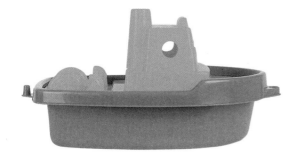
boat

road

toad

soap

Say the words: boat, road, toad, soap.

Ai sounds

Look at the sound in the blue box. Trace the sound, then find it in the words below by underlining it.

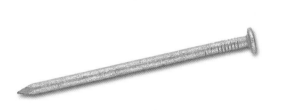

nail

train

rain

Which words rhyme?

sail

Say the words: nail, train, rain, sail.

Numbers
1-50

Are you ready to learn your numbers?

1

one dinosaur

look at the number   **start**   trace the number   draw inside

Practice writing the number **1**.

Now write it yourself.

1 grass cutter

1 hen

1 barn

1 pig

one one

Can you match the baby to its mother?

foal

sheep

calf

cow

lamb

horse

2

two motorcycles

 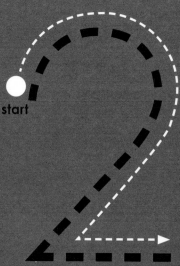 

look at the number   trace the number   draw inside

start

Practice writing the number **2**.

Now write it yourself.

Follow the instructions carefully to draw the number.

2 lemons

2 strawberries

2 bananas

2 apples

two two

How many cherries are there?

How many melon slices are there?

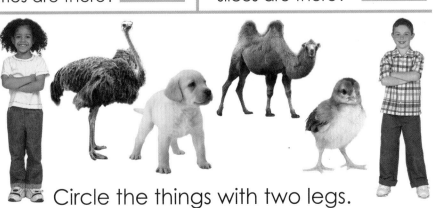

Circle the things with two legs.

Circle the two fruits that are the same.

3

three cars

 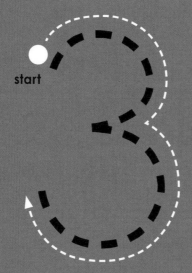 

start

look at the number   trace the number   draw inside

Practice writing the number **3**.

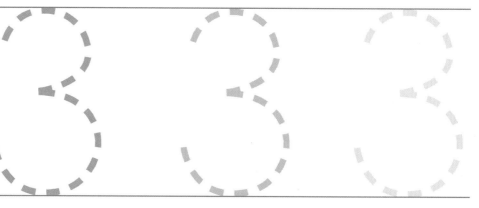

Now write it yourself.

Keep your tracing between the lines!

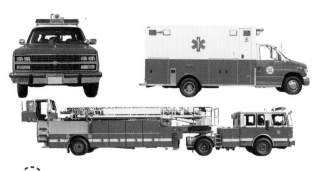

3 emergency vehicles

3 trucks

3 tractors

3 diggers

threethree

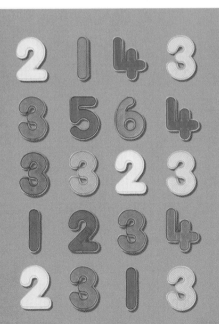

Circle each
number 3.

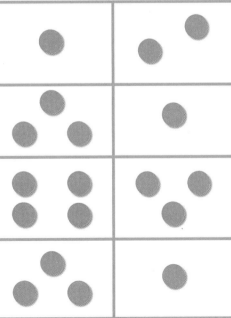

Circle the groups
of three dots.

Circle the shapes
with three sides.

4

four cows

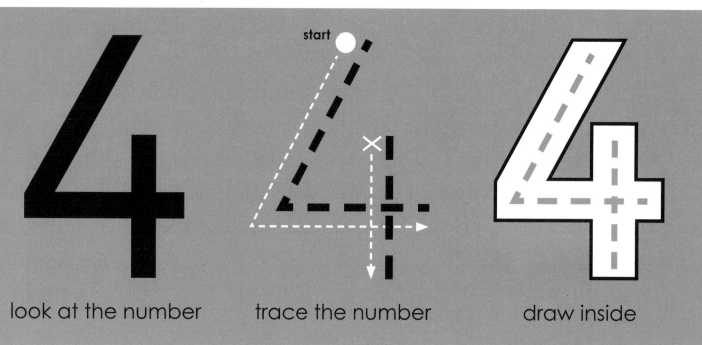

look at the number

trace the number

start

draw inside

Practice writing the number **4**

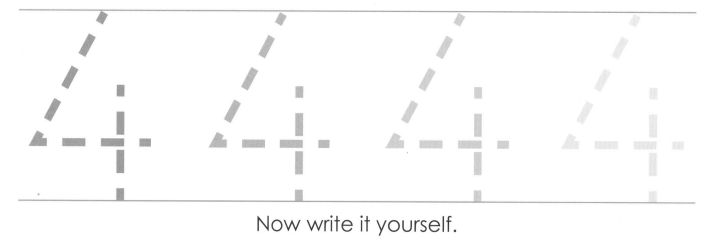

Now write it yourself.

four four

4 party dresses

4 kids at a party

4 presents

4 balloons

How many popsicles? ☐

How many cupcakes? ☐

Circle the four blue candies.

Circle the things with four legs.

5

five dolls

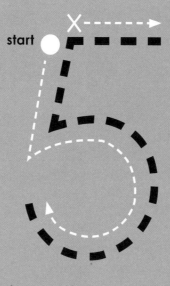

look at the number   trace the number   draw inside

Practice writing the number **5**.

Now write it yourself.

five five

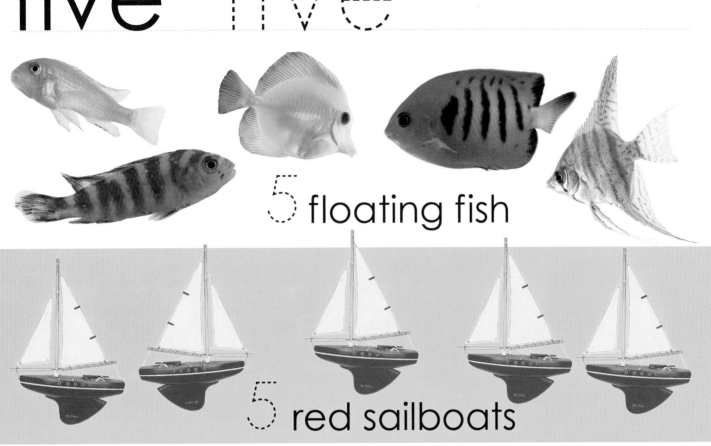

5 floating fish

5 red sailboats

Connect the stars with five points.

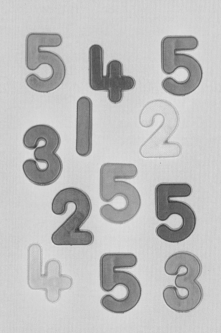

Circle each number 5.

Circle the five yellow chicks.

6

six horses

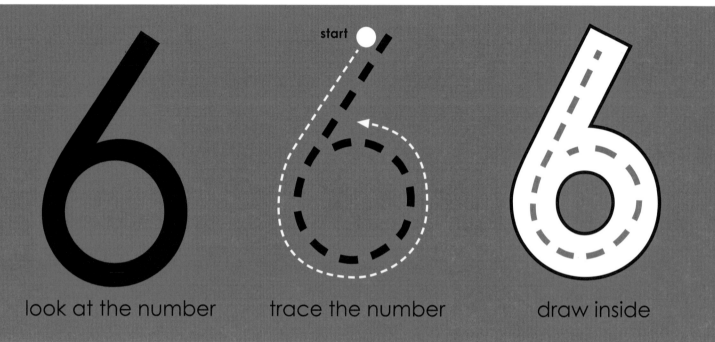

look at the number   trace the number   draw inside

Practice writing the number **6**.

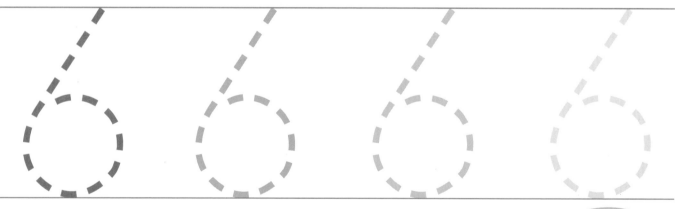

Now write it yourself.

Keep going. You are doing really well!

6 frogs

6 butterflies

6 dragonflies

6 snakes

six six

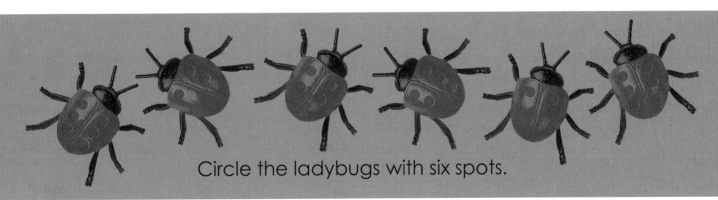

Circle the ladybugs with six spots.

Circle the bugs with six legs.

7

seven puppies

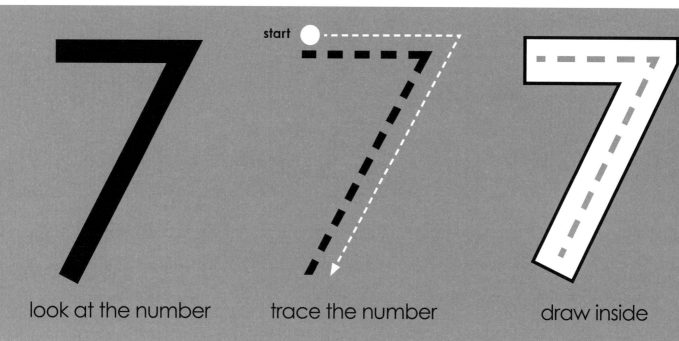

start

look at the number

trace the number

draw inside

Practice writing the number **7**.

Now write it yourself.

How many puppies are eating?

seven seven

7 girls

7 boys

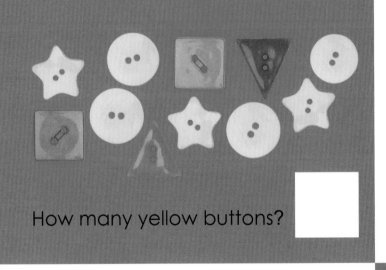

How many yellow buttons? ▢

How many hats? ▢

Circle each number 7.

Connect each number 7.

8

eight vegetables

 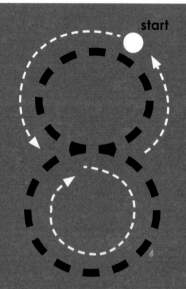 

8	8	8
look at the number	trace the number	draw inside

start

Practice writing the number **8**.

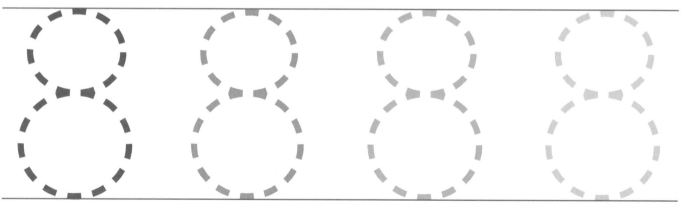

Now write it yourself.

8 puppies

8 kittens

eight eight

Circle the toy with eight legs.

Circle the eight green things.

How many birds are there?

9

nine fruits

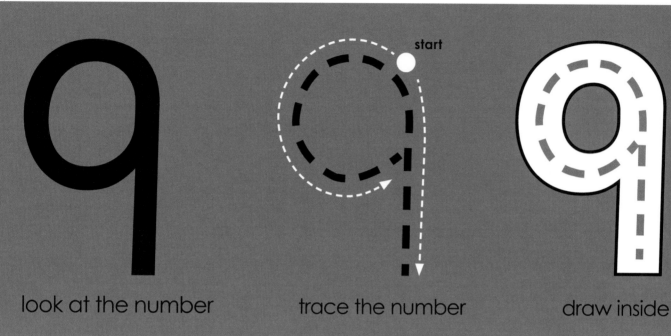

look at the number

trace the number

start

draw inside

Practice writing the number **9**.

Now write it yourself.

9 triangles

9 coins

9 decorations

9 gift bows

nine nine

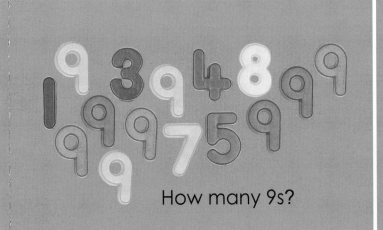

How many 9s?

How many flowers?

Circle the T-shirts with number 9.

10

ten kittens

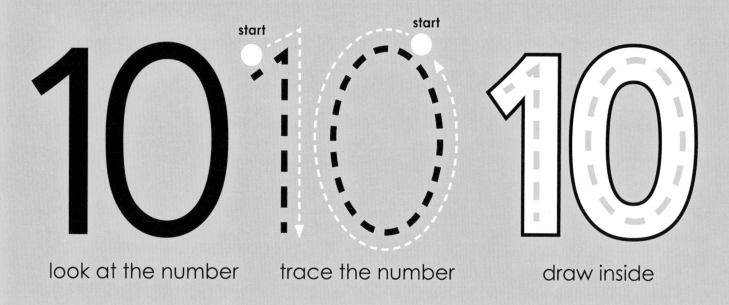

start

start

look at the number

trace the number

draw inside

Practice writing the number **10**.

Now write it yourself.

How many kittens are in the basket?

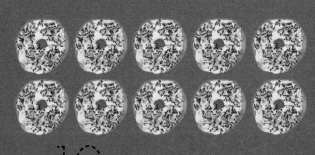

10 candies

10 donuts

10 chocolate eggs

ten ten

How many ice creams?

How many brown animals?

Circle the number 10 car.

11

eleven fish

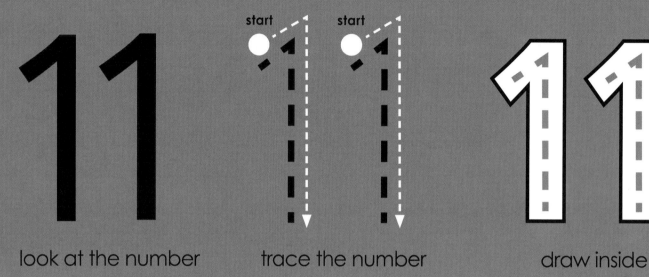

11
look at the number

start start
trace the number

draw inside

Practice writing the number **11**.

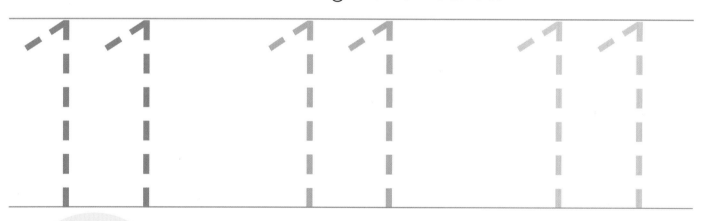

Now write it yourself.

Remember what you have learned before!

12

twelve teddy bears

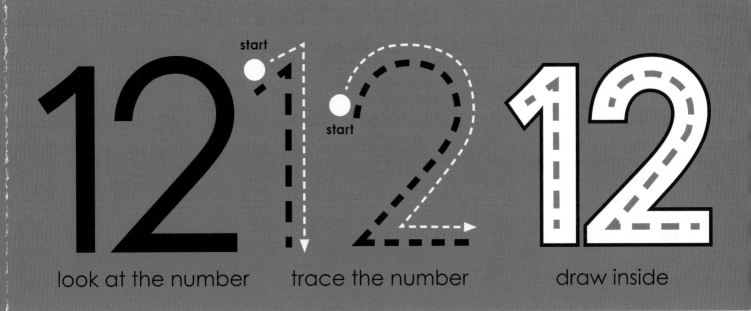

look at the number   trace the number   draw inside

Practice writing the number **12**.

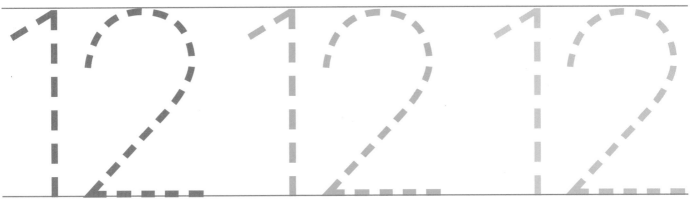

Now write it yourself.

13

thirteen chicks

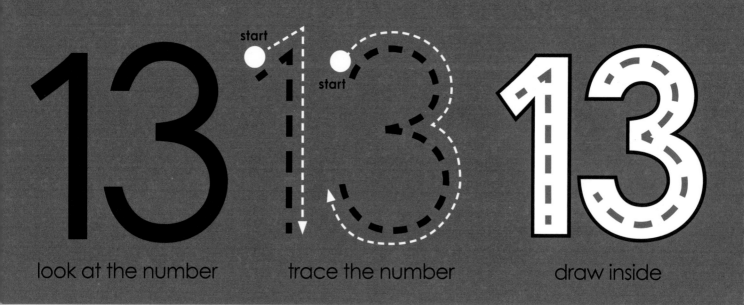

look at the number

trace the number

draw inside

Practice writing the number **13**.

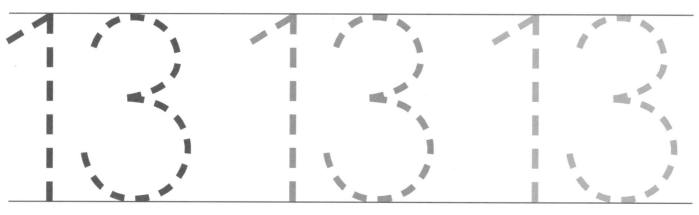

Now write it yourself.

14

fourteen hats

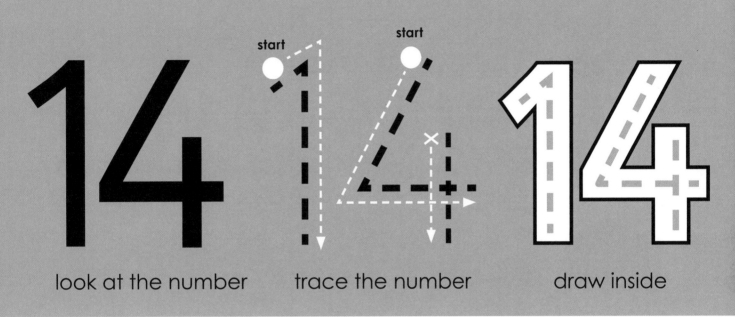

look at the number

start

trace the number

×

draw inside

Practice writing the number **14**.

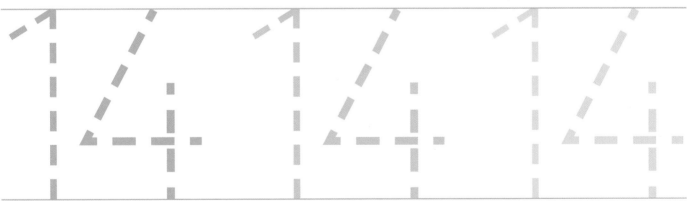

Now write it yourself.

Circle the pirate hat in the picture above.

15

fifteen leaves

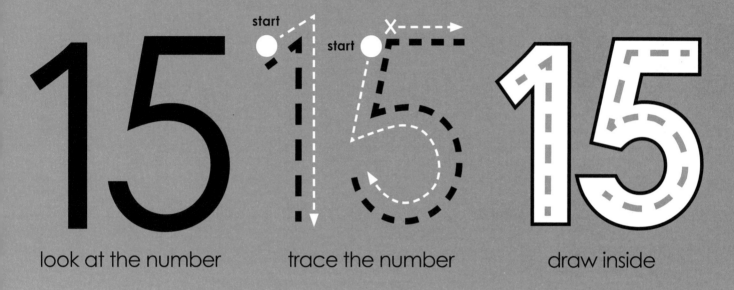

look at the number

start

start

X

trace the number

draw inside

Practice writing the number **15**.

Now write it yourself.

How many green leaves can you count?

16

sixteen balloons

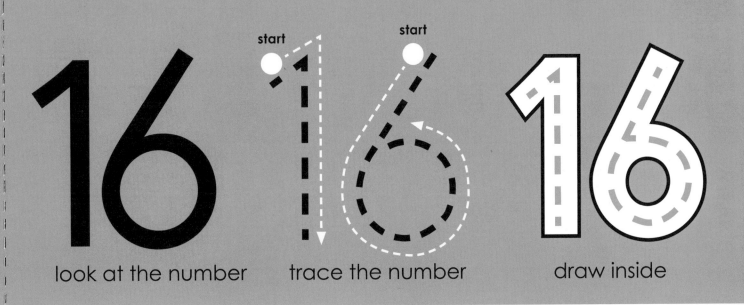

look at the number

trace the number

draw inside

Practice writing the number **16**.

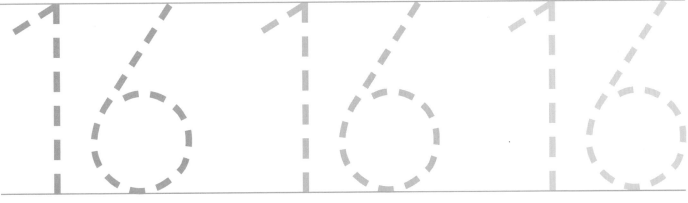

Now write it yourself.

17

seventeen flowers

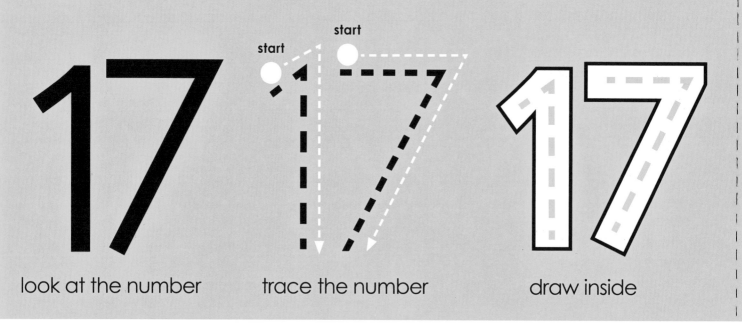

look at the number   trace the number   draw inside

Practice writing the number **17**.

Now write it yourself.

18

eighteen candies

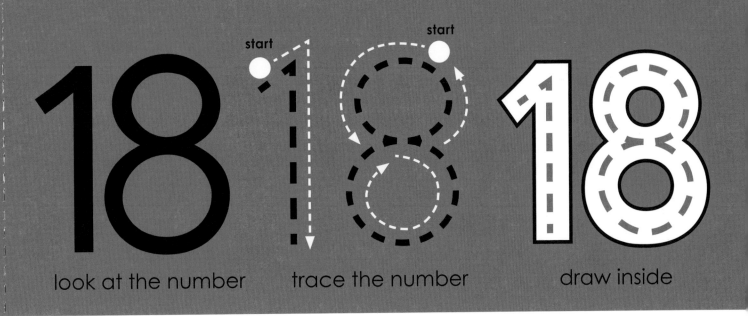

look at the number   trace the number   draw inside

Practice writing the number **18**.

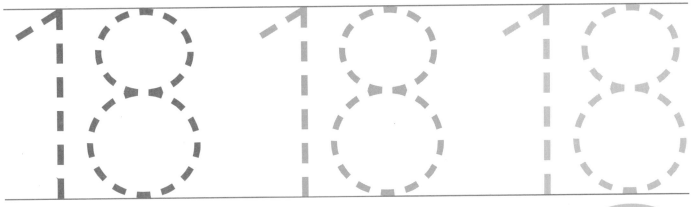

Now write it yourself.

Remember to trace the numbers first!

19

nineteen balls

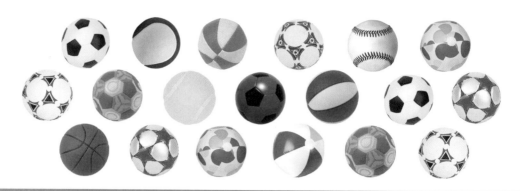

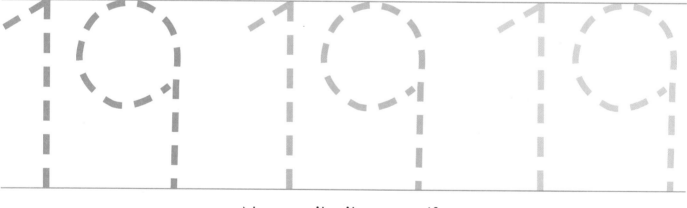

look at the number

start

trace the number

start

draw inside

Practice writing the number **19**.

Now write it yourself.

20

twenty ducks

 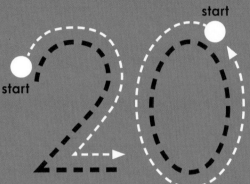 

look at the number   trace the number   draw inside

Practice writing the number **20**.

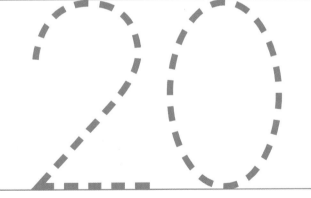

Now write it yourself.

Why don't you practice what you have learned?

11-15

Count the items and write the numbers.

11 floaties

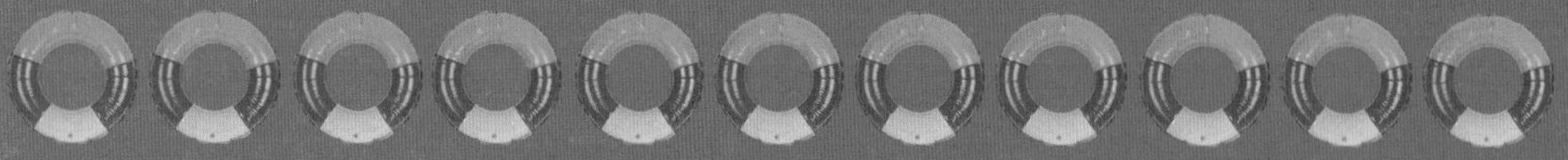

$=$ 11

12 penguins

$=$ 12

13 leaves

$=$ 13

14 cherries

$=$ 14

15 flamingos

$=$ 15

16-20

Circle the item in each group that is different and write the numbers.

16 socks

 = 16

17 paw prints

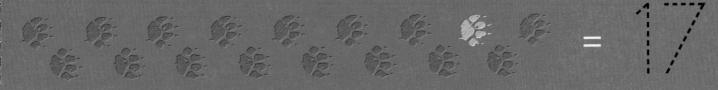 = 17

18 flowers

= 18

19 pencils

 = 19

20 peas

 = 20

High numbers

Trace and practice numbers 21 to 25.

High numbers

Trace and practice numbers 26 to 30.

There are 28 days in February, but 29 if it's a leap year!

High numbers

Trace and practice numbers 31 to 35.

Time yourself counting from 1 to 35. How long did you take?

High numbers

Trace and practice numbers 36 to 40.

High numbers

Trace and practice numbers 41 to 45.

High numbers

Trace and practice numbers 46 to 50.

Good work! You've learned numbers 1 to 50!

10

Number Skills

Now let's learn about adding and subtracting!

Number pairs

Using your pen or pencil, trace the numbers below.
Follow the direction of the arrows.

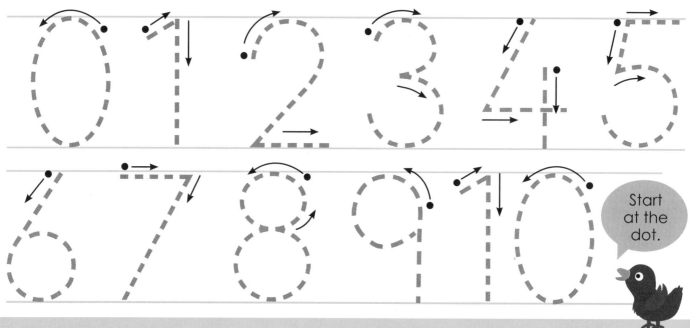

Here are pairs of numbers that when added
together make 10. Now try to trace them.

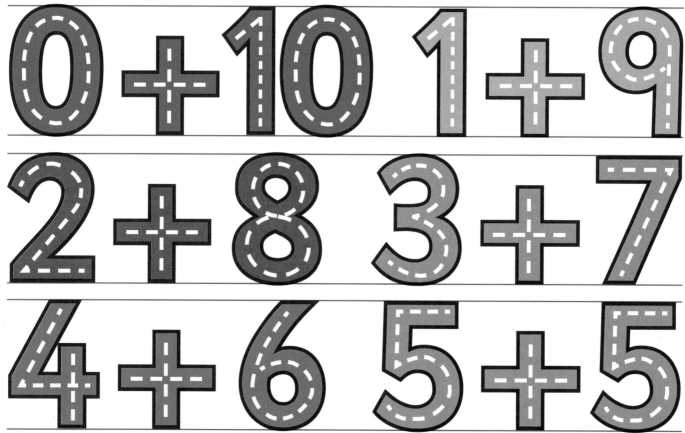

0 + 10 = 10

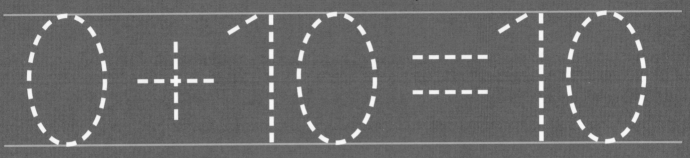

Count the children and complete the sum below.

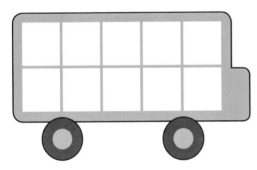  

 children + children = children

This pig is missing 10 mud splatters.

Can you draw 10 mud splatters on the pig?

Practice this number pair.

 **+**  **= 10**

229

1 + 9 = 10

Trace this number pair.

Count the children and complete the sum below.

 child + children = 10 children

It is Sarah's birthday.
She will be 10.

Can you draw the missing candles on her cake to make 10?

Practice this number pair.

☐ **+** ☐ **=10**

2 + 8 = 10

Trace this number pair.

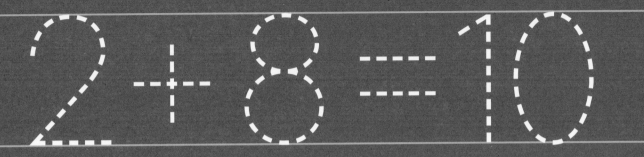

2 + 8 = 10

Count the children and complete the sum below.

2 children + 8 children = 10 children

This pizza is missing some pieces of pepperoni.

Can you draw the missing pepperoni to make 10 pieces?

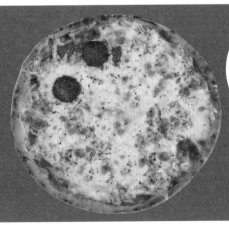

Count the number of pieces on the pizza to start with!

Practice this number pair.

☐ **+** ☐ **=10**

3 + 7 = 10

Trace this number pair.

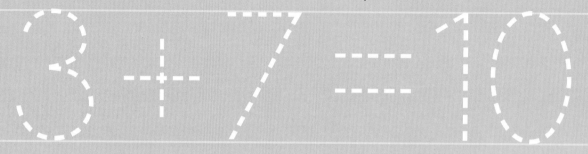

Count the children and complete the sum below.

$\boxed{3}$ children + $\boxed{7}$ children = $\boxed{10}$ children

Only some of the wizards' hats have stars!

Can you draw the missing stars to make 10?

Practice this number pair.

$\boxed{}$  $\boxed{}$ $= 10$

232

4 + 6 = 10

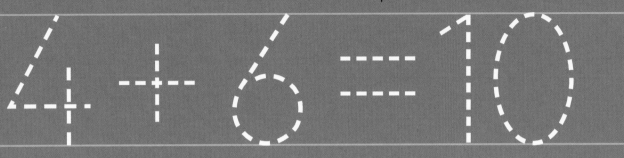

Count the children and complete the sum below.

$\boxed{4}$ children + $\boxed{6}$ children = $\boxed{10}$ children

Danny the dinosaur is missing some spikes.

Can you draw his missing spikes to make 10?

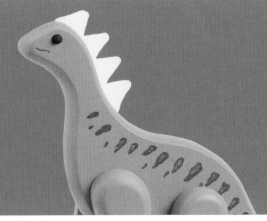

Practice this number pair.

$\boxed{}$ **+** $\boxed{}$ **= 10**

5 + 5 = 10

Trace this number pair.

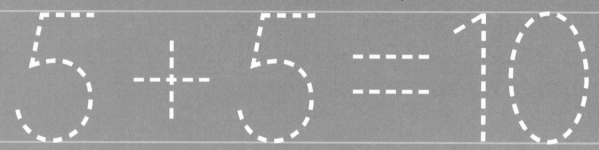

Count the children and complete the sum below.

 children + children = 10 children

This ladybug is missing some spots.

Can you draw the missing spots to make 10?

Practice this number pair.

 +  = 10

Pairs reversed

Did you know that 0 + 10 = 10 is the same as 10 + 0 = 10?
Each pair can be written in two ways.

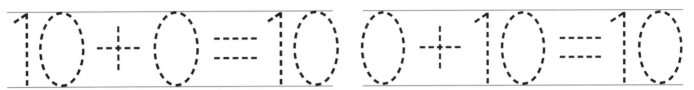

Can you see the pattern?

Trace each pair and its answer.

10 + 0 = 10	0 + 10 = 10
9 + 1 = 10	1 + 9 = 10
8 + 2 = 10	2 + 8 = 10
7 + 3 = 10	3 + 7 = 10
6 + 4 = 10	4 + 6 = 10
5 + 5 = 10	5 + 5 = 10

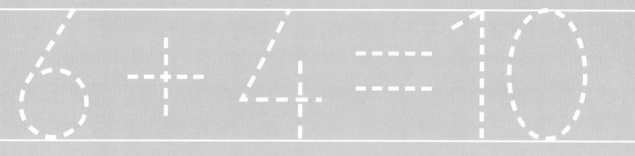

6 + 4 = 10

Count the children and complete the sum below.

 children + children = children

Bill's dinner plate is missing some peas.

Can you draw the missing peas to make 10?

Practice this number pair.

 +  = 10

7 + 3 = 10

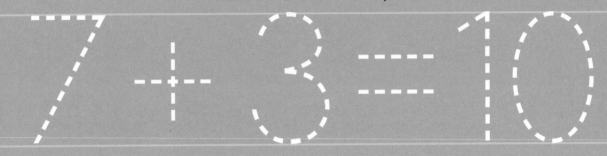

Count the children and complete the sum below.

7 children + 3 children = 10 children

This garden should have 10 flowers.

Can you draw the missing flowers to make 10?

Practice this number pair. ☐ + ☐ = 10

8 + 2 = 10

Trace this number pair.

Count the children and complete the sum below.

8 children + 2 children = 10 children

Some cupcakes are missing their strawberries.

Can you draw the missing strawberries to make 10?

Practice this number pair.  **+**  **=10**

9 + 1 = 10

Count the children and complete the sum below.

9 children + 1 child = 10 children

This frog needs to get across the pond.

Can you draw the 1 missing lily pad to make 10?

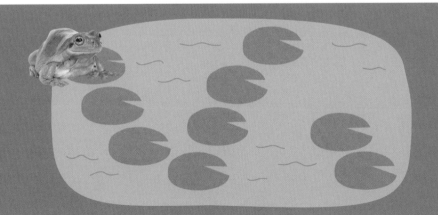

Practice this number pair.

☐ + ☐ = 10

239

10 + 0 = 10

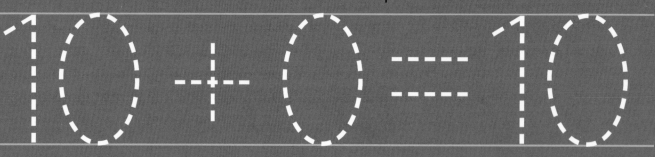

Count the children and complete the sum below.

 children + children = children

How many jewels are there on the crown?

Circle all the jewels in the crown to make 10.

Practice this number pair. ☐ **+** ☐ **= 10**

240

Octopus math

Ollie Octopus loves the number 10. Can you write
the number pairs of 10 on his long legs?

Adding 1

Add **1** to the first group of objects to find the totals.
Write the numbers in the boxes.

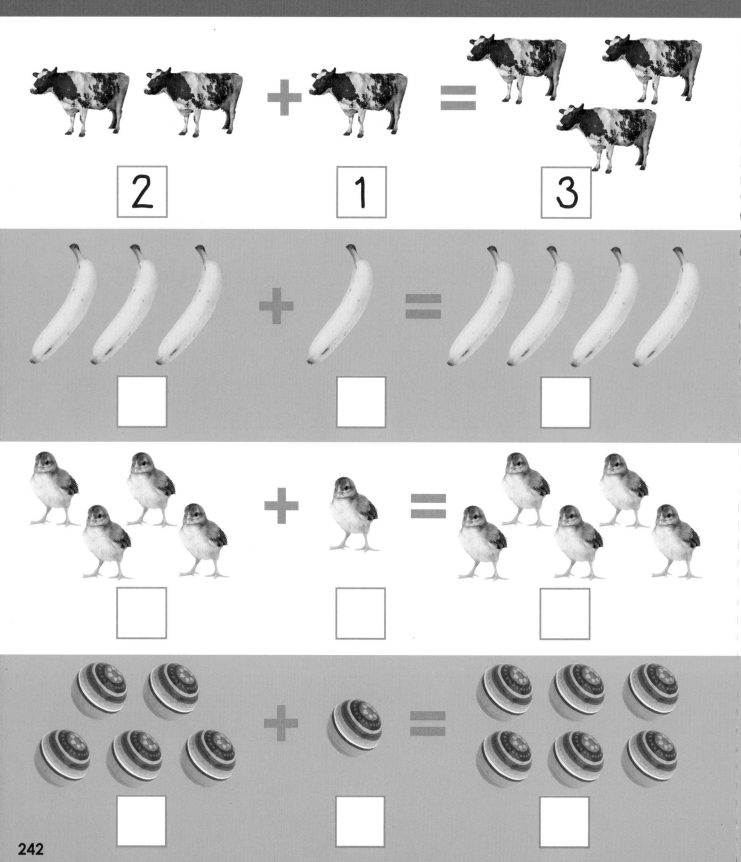

2 + 1 = 3

Subtracting 1

Subtract **1** from the first group of objects to find the totals.
Write the numbers in the boxes.

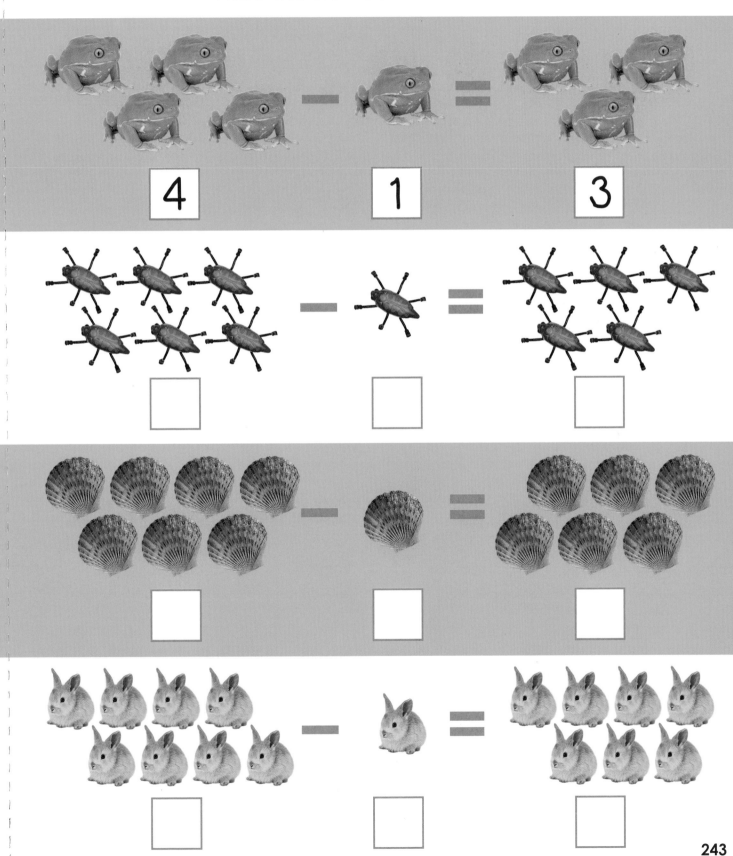

Adding groups

Write the amount of each group in the boxes.
Then add the groups together.

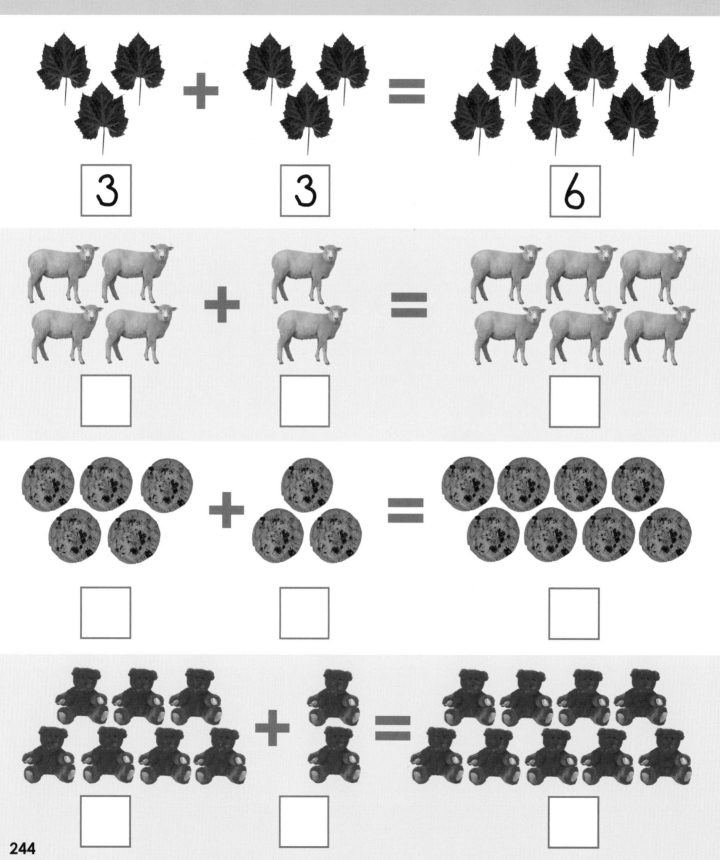

Subtracting groups

Write the amount of each group in the boxes.
Subtract the second group from the first.

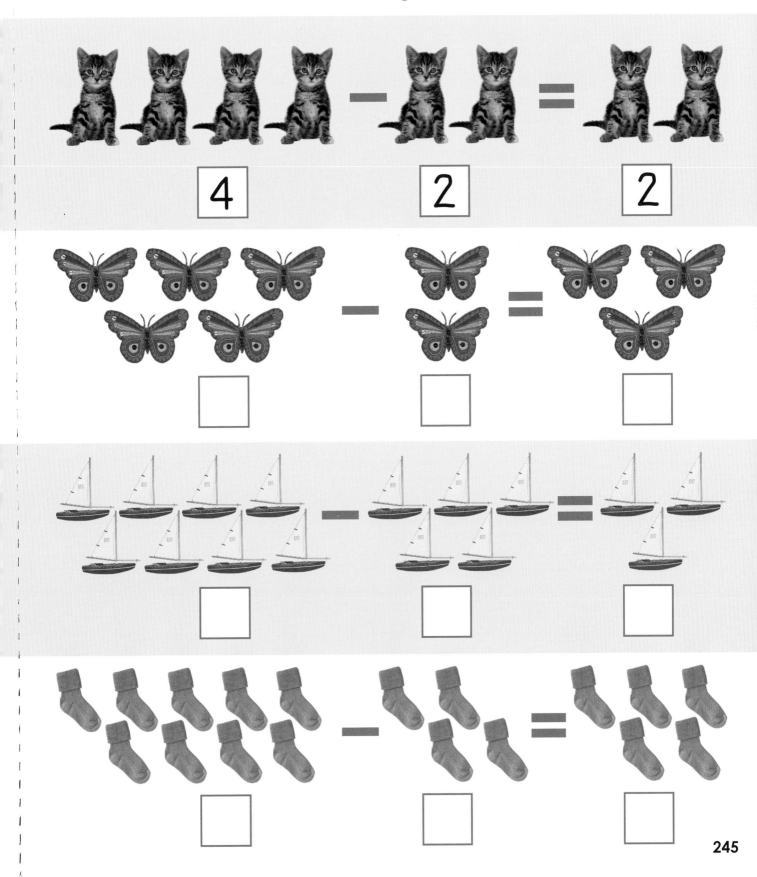

245

Subtracting to 5

Try these different ways of subtracting to make 5.

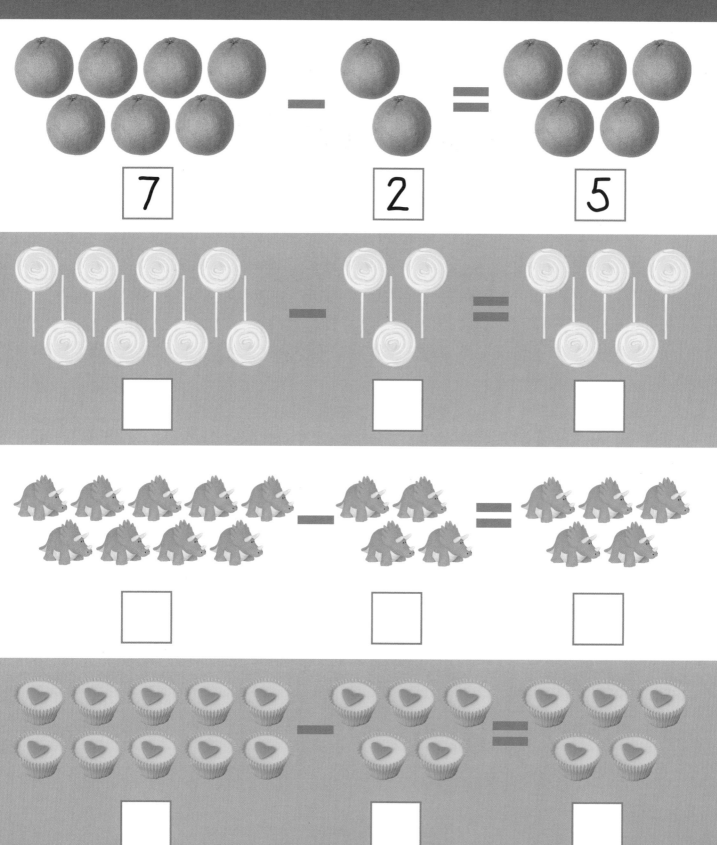

7 − 2 = 5

Adding to 10

Try these different ways of adding to make 10.

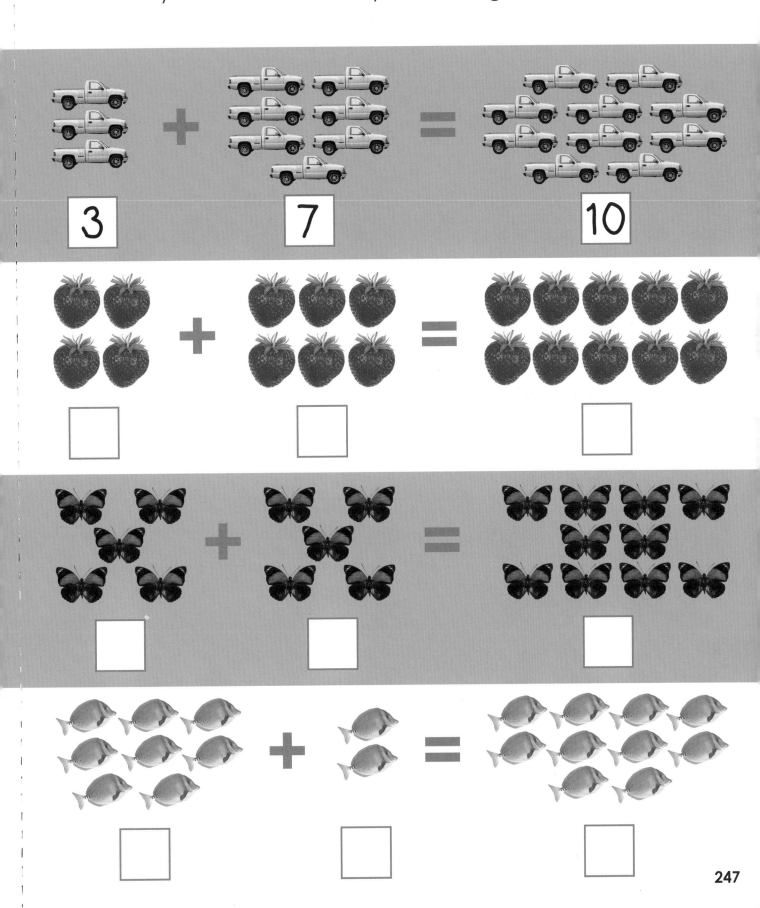

Doubling numbers

To double a number, add the same number onto itself.

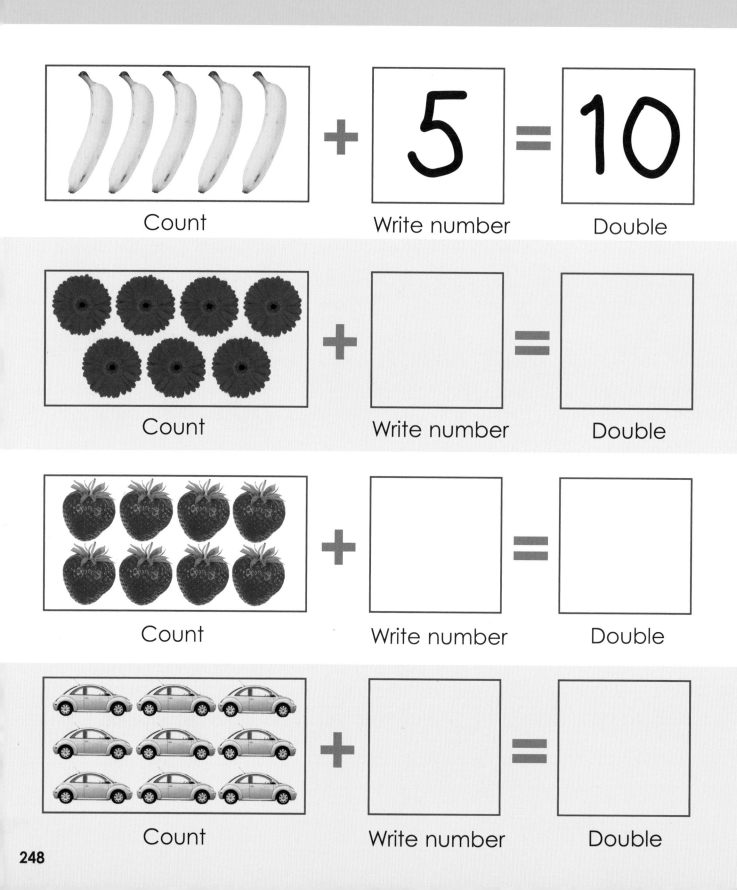

Count + Write number **5** = Double **10**

Count + Write number = Double

Count + Write number = Double

Count + Write number = Double

Halving numbers

When you halve a number, the amount you take away is the same number that is left over.

Cross out the objects to make

half of 4

 $= \boxed{2}$

Cross out the objects to make

half of 6

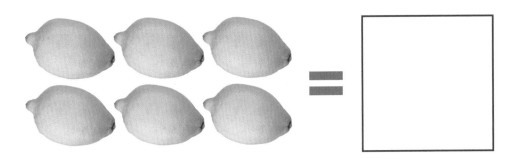 $= \boxed{}$

Cross out the objects to make

half of 8

 $= \boxed{}$

Cross out the objects to make

half of 10

$= \boxed{}$

Addition
using number pairs

Use the number pairs of 10 to solve these problems.
Write the missing numbers in the boxes.

$4 + \boxed{} = 10$

$\boxed{} + 9 = 10$

$\boxed{} + 7 = 10$

Practice the sums first!

$5 + \boxed{} = 10$

$2 + \boxed{} = 10$

$0 + \boxed{} = 10$

Construction pairs

Draw lines between the two cranes to match up the number pairs of 10. The first one is done for you.

Galaxy challenge

Can you solve these intergalactic calculations?

9 − 5 =

6 − 4 =

4 + 5 =

8 + 1 =

2 + 6 =

Blast off!

Now try these subtraction calculations.

$8 - 4 =$ ▢

$9 - 6 =$ ▢

$7 - 5 =$ ▢

$4 - 3 =$ ▢

253

Counting food

Count how many pieces of food are on each plate
and write the answer in the box below.

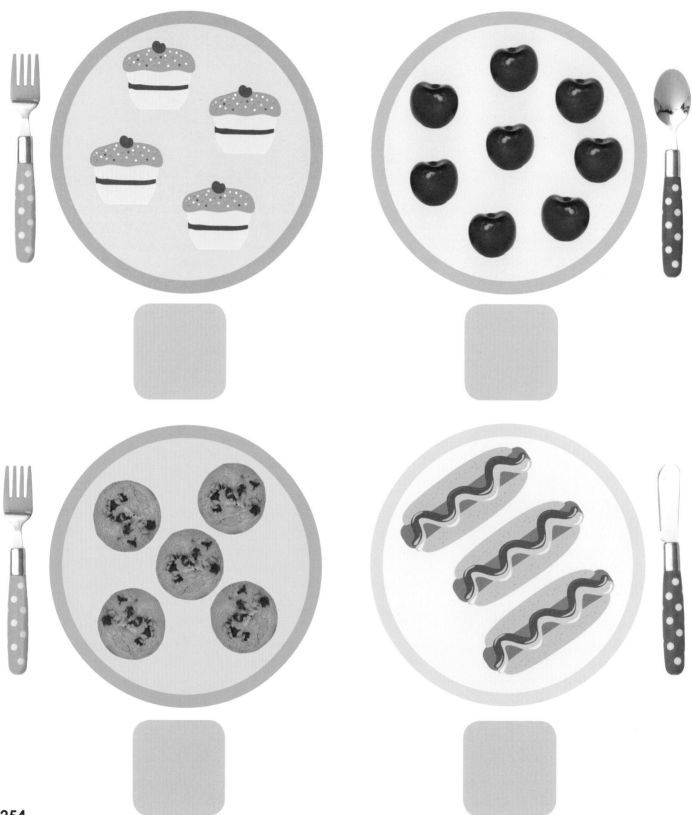

More or less

Can you solve these number problems?
Use the number line to help you.

1 2 3 4 5 6 7 8 9 10

Circle the numbers that are less than 5.

5 (2) 9 3 7 1 4

Circle the numbers that are more than 3.

3 1 4 8 2 7 9

Circle the numbers that are less than 4.

4 9 1 7 3 2 6

1 to 20

There are 20 flowers to count.
Fill in the missing numbers to complete the sequence.

Number grid

Which numbers are bigger than 10?
Find them in the grid and circle them.

3	17	6	11	15	5	6	10
16	2	12	1	16	3	8	4
9	15	20	3	1	(11)	1	18
19	7	1	14	8	10	3	17
10	3	11	6	13	19	15	2
1	5	9	4	1	3	11	16
15	12	3	20	7	12	8	12
4	20	13	16	1	19	13	5

Copy the example.

257

Number match

How many butterflies are in each cloud?
Draw a line from each cloud to the flower with the answer.

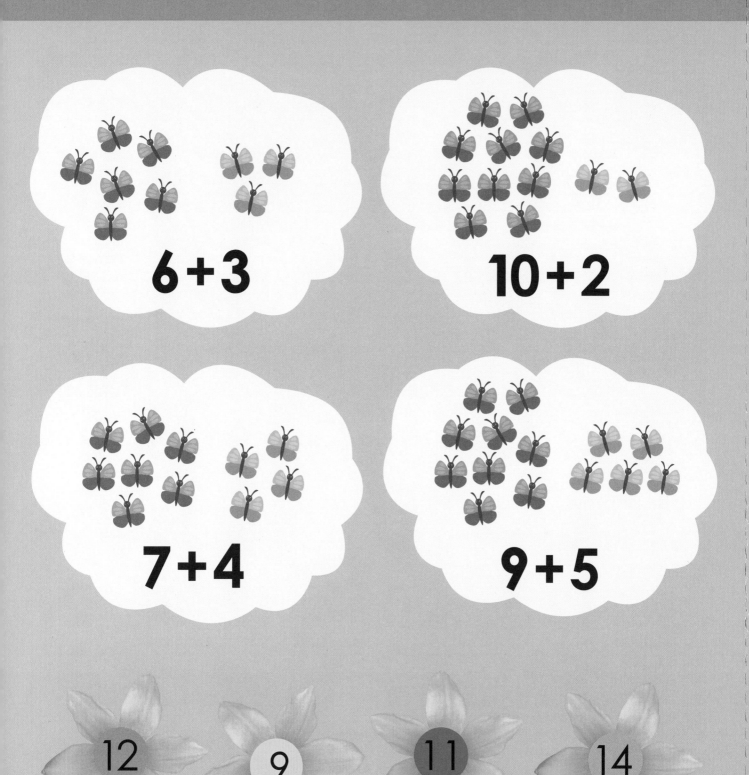

6+3

10+2

7+4

9+5

12

9

11

14

Tiger puzzles

Can you solve these subtraction calculations?

7 - 2 =

9 - 4 =

8 - 2 =

10 - 3 =

15 - 5 =

You can do it!

Matching socks

Draw lines between the socks that
make number pairs of 10.

Bone hunt

Can you match the dogs and their bones to their doghouses using the number pairs of 10?

Subtraction
using number pairs

Number pairs can be used to help you solve problems involving subtraction from 10. Trace over the subtractions.

10 - 0 = 10	10 - 5 = 5
10 - 1 = 9	10 - 6 = 4
10 - 2 = 8	10 - 7 = 3
10 - 3 = 7	10 - 8 = 2
10 - 4 = 6	10 - 9 = 1

Can you see the pattern?

What is the answer to the problem below? Use the number pairs above to help.

10 - 2 =

Crazy crabs

Can you solve these subtraction problems by writing in the missing numbers?

10 − ☐ = 7

10 − ☐ = 1

10 − ☐ = 6

10 − ☐ = 2

10 − ☐ = 10

Caterpillar puzzles

These poor caterpillars should have 10 shoes on their feet.
Can you work out how many they are missing?

Benny has only 6 shoes.
How many is he missing?

$$10 - 6 = \boxed{}$$

Sophie has only 2 shoes.
How many is she missing?

$$10 - 2 = \boxed{}$$

Joe has only 5 shoes.
How many is he missing?

$$10 - 5 = \boxed{}$$

Number pairs

Follow the instructions to make number pairs of 10
and write your answers in the boxes below.

Count the butterflies. How many
more butterflies make 10?

Count the lambs. How many
more lambs make 10?

Telling Time

I'm here to help!

Let's learn to tell time!

The clock

Trace the numbers on the clock face.

A clock face shows 12 hours.

The hands move this way around the clock.

The long hand tells you the minutes.

The short hand tells you the hour.

People use clocks to tell time.

Tell time

Can you draw a long hand and a short hand on the clock face?

Where does the short hand go when it is 8 o'clock?

Use the clock on the left to help you.

O'clock

When the long hand points to the 12, it is something o'clock.

The time is 2 o'clock!

On this clock, the long hand is pointing to the **12** and the short hand is pointing to the **2**. The time is **2** o'clock.

1 o'clock

2 o'clock

3 o'clock

Trace the clock hands on the clocks above.

What time is it?

Draw the clock hands to show the time on the clocks.
The first three are done for you.

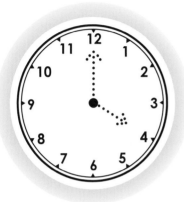

4 o'clock

5 o'clock

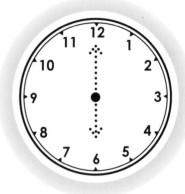

6 o'clock

7 o'clock

8 o'clock

9 o'clock

10 o'clock

11 o'clock

12 o'clock

My day

Draw the short hands.

Trace the long hands then fill in the clocks with
what time you do these activities.

I wake up at _____ o'clock
in the morning.

Breakfast is at _____ o'clock
in the morning.

School starts at _____ o'clock
in the morning.

I eat lunch at _____ o'clock
in the morning.

My day

Fill in the clocks with what time you do these activities.

Playtime is at _____ o'clock
in the afternoon.

Dinner is at _____ o'clock
in the afternoon.

Bathtime is at _____ o'clock
in the evening.

Bedtime is at _____ o'clock
in the evening.

5-minute steps

When the long hand reaches a number, it means that it is a number of minutes after the hour.

Trace the numbers.

On this clock, the long hand is pointing to the **1**. The short hand is just after **9**. The time is 5 minutes after **9**.

5-minute steps

Trace the clock hands and write the times shown on the clocks.

___5___ after 12   _____ after 12   _____ after 12

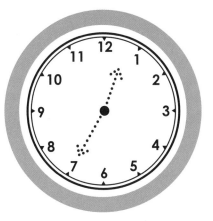 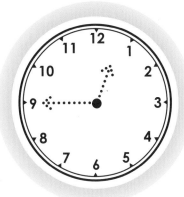 

_____ after 12   _____ after 12   _____ after 12

 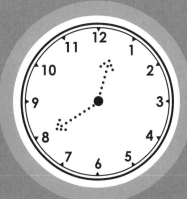 

_____ after 12   _____ after 12   _____ after 12

Talking time

Between 30 minutes and o'clock, instead of saying "minutes after," we can say the time as "minutes to."

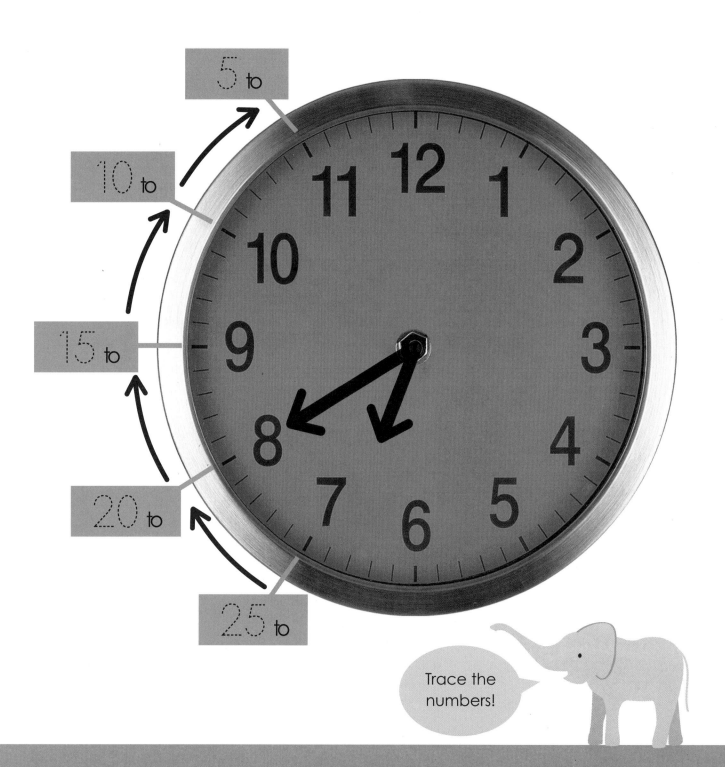

5 to

10 to

15 to

20 to

25 to

Trace the numbers!

On this clock, the long hand is pointing to the 8. The short hand is just before 7. The time is 20 minutes to 7.

Talking time

Following the example, draw the long hands on the clocks to show the minutes to the hour.

25 to 8

5 to 7

25 to 11

10 to 2

20 to 12

15 to 9

10 to 7

15 to 6

25 to 3

Half past the hour

When the long hand points to 6, it is 30 minutes past the hour.

Trace the numbers leading up to 30 minutes.

On this clock, the long hand is pointing to the 6. The short hand is halfway between the 12 and 1. The time is 12 thirty.

What is the time?

Look at each clock below, then write down
the time shown on the line underneath it.

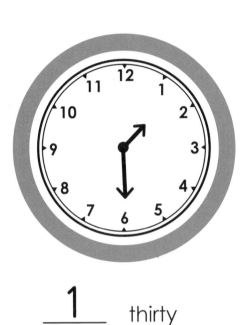

__1__ thirty

_____ thirty

_____ thirty

_____ thirty

Starting with 1 thirty, join a line between
the clocks to show the correct order of time.

Quarter after the hour

When the long hand points to the 3, it is 15 minutes past the hour. This is the same as quarter after the hour.

Trace the numbers leading up to quarter after.

On this clock, the long hand is pointing to the 3. The short hand is a quarter of the way between the 6 and the 7. The time is a quarter after 6.

Talking time

Write the "quarter after" times shown on the clocks.

quarter after _____

quarter after _____

quarter after _____

quarter after _____

quarter after _____

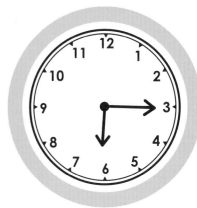

quarter after _____

quarter after _____

quarter after _____

quarter after _____

Quarter to the hour

When the long hand points to the 9, it is 15 minutes to the hour. This is the same as quarter to the hour.

Trace the numbers leading from quarter to the hour.

On this clock, the long hand is pointing to the 9. The short hand is three quarters of the way between the 6 and the 7. The time is a quarter to 7.

Talking time

Complete the clocks and show the correct times below.

quarter to 2

quarter to 12

quarter to 6

quarter to _____

quarter to _____

quarter to _____

quarter to 3

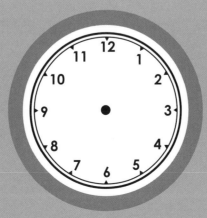

quarter to 9

quarter to 8

Digital clock

Clocks that use only numbers to tell the time are called digital clocks.

The clock is showing 5 o'clock

On a digital clock, it is shown as 5:00.

5:00

Digital time

Trace over the numbers on the digital clocks.

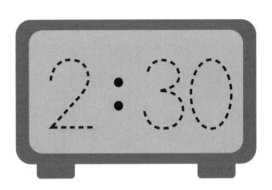

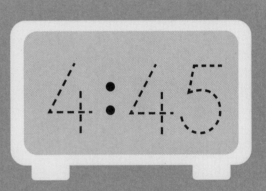

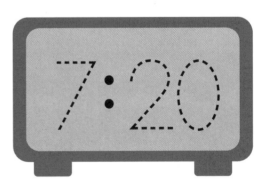

285

Alarm clocks

Draw a line to match the times on the clocks to the digital clocks.

Alarm clocks

Trace the numbers!

Draw the hands on the clocks to match the time shown on the digital clocks.

What time is it?

Fill in the clocks with the correct times.

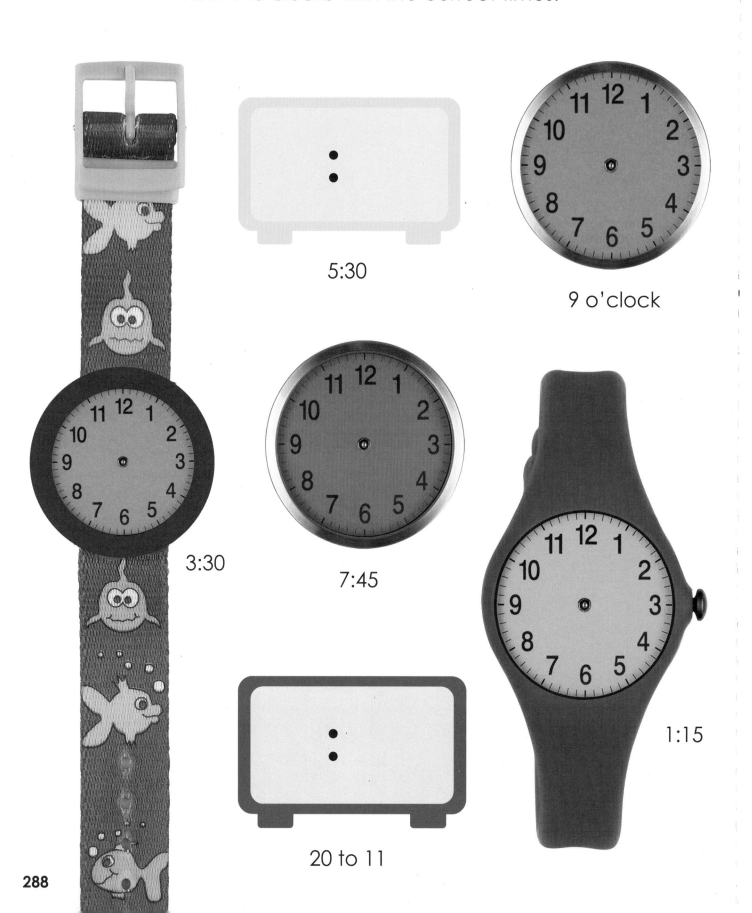

5:30

9 o'clock

3:30

7:45

1:15

20 to 11

What time is it?

Fill in the clocks with the correct times.

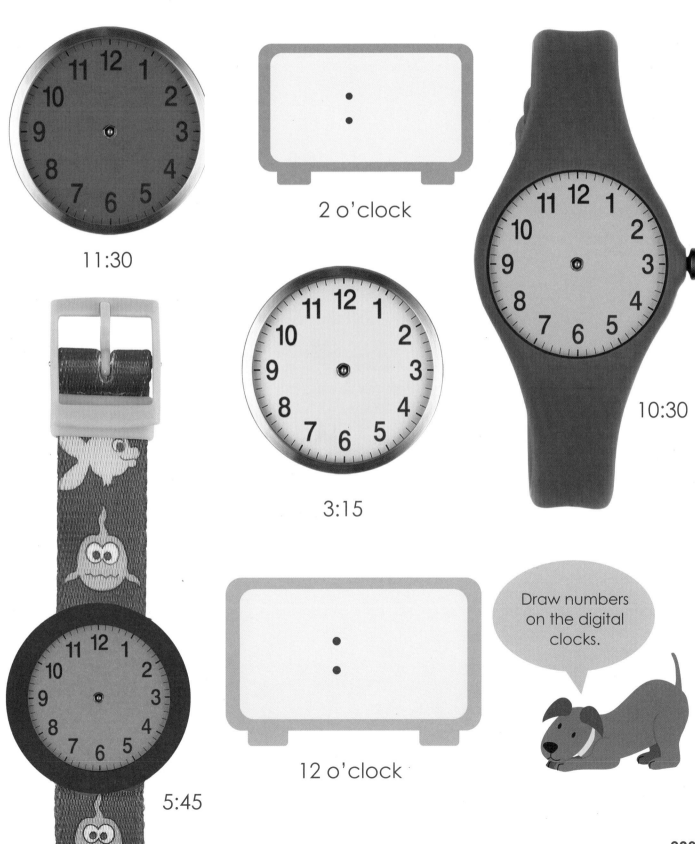

11:30

2 o'clock

10:30

3:15

5:45

12 o'clock

Draw numbers on the digital clocks.

Race time

Today is race day. Fill out the clocks with the times the different horses start their races.

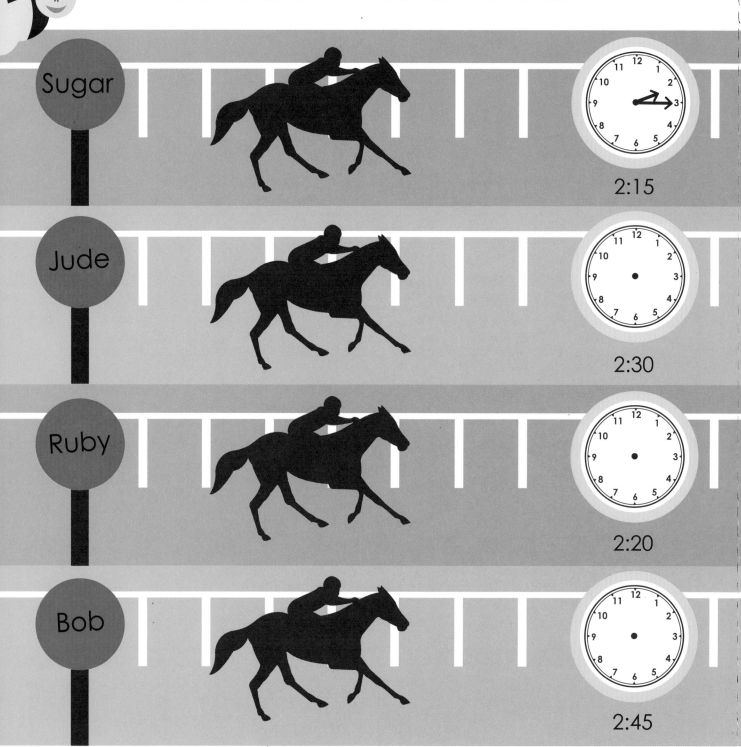

Sugar — 2:15

Jude — 2:30

Ruby — 2:20

Bob — 2:45

Who was the first and the last to start their race?

first to start _____   last to start _____

Airport

Trace the digital clock times on the airport departures board.

London	7:20
Dublin	7:45
New York	8:59

What time does the flight depart for Madrid? _____
Which flight departs at 7:20? _____

Draw on the clocks below to show the flight departure times:

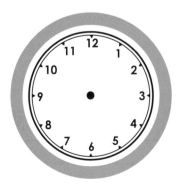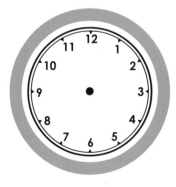

Dublin

New York

Paris

Times of day

Noon happens at 12 o'clock in the afternoon.
Midnight happens at 12 o'clock at night.

Show noon on the clock.

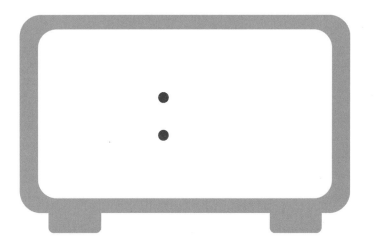

Show midnight on the digital clock.

It is **4** hours after noon. What time is it?
It is **4** hours before midnight. What time is it?

Sunrise and sunset

In the summer, the sun rises early in the morning and sets late in the evening. What time did the sun rise and set?

Sunrise _____

Sunset _____

In the winter, the sun rises later in the morning and sets earlier in the evening. What time did the sun rise and set?

Sunrise _____

Sunset _____

In the summer, daytime is longer.
In the winter, nighttime is longer.

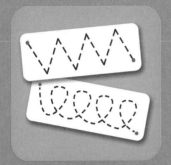

Let's Get Ready for School

Now let's get ready for school with lots of fun activities!

Odd one out

Following the example, circle the animal in each group that does not belong.

Circle the animal that is not a pet.

Circle the animal that is not an insect.

Circle the animal that is not wild.

Circle the animal that does not live under the sea.

Animal families

Draw a line between the barnyard moms and their babies.

cow

What other animals can you find on a farm?

sheep

duck

calf

lamb

duckling

People who help us

Draw a line between the workers and
the vehicles they use in their jobs.

firefighter

ambulance

Can you think of any other jobs people do?

doctor

school bus

teacher

fire truck

Big and small

Circle the answers to the
questions in the pictures below.

Which building is the biggest?

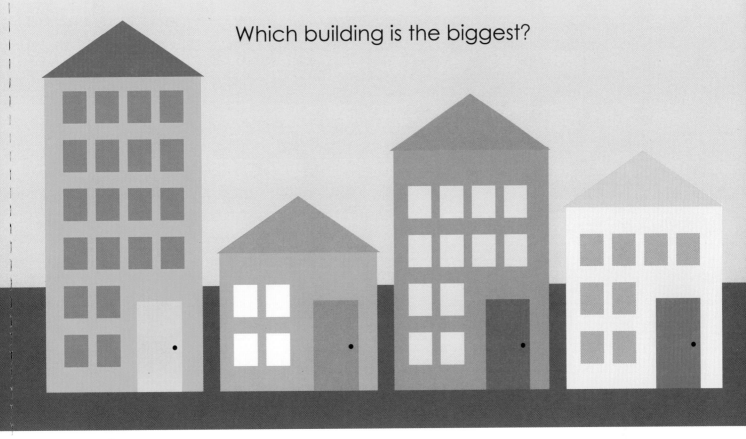

Which flower is the smallest?

Bright colors

Learn your colors by tracing over the color names below.

red green

yellow

pink

blue

What's your favorite color?

The cat is the color

orange.

Counting colors

Write the number of different-colored toys
on each shelf in the boxes below.

Follow the example!

1
blue

red

green

yellow

Tracing shapes

Trace along the dotted lines of
each of the shapes below.

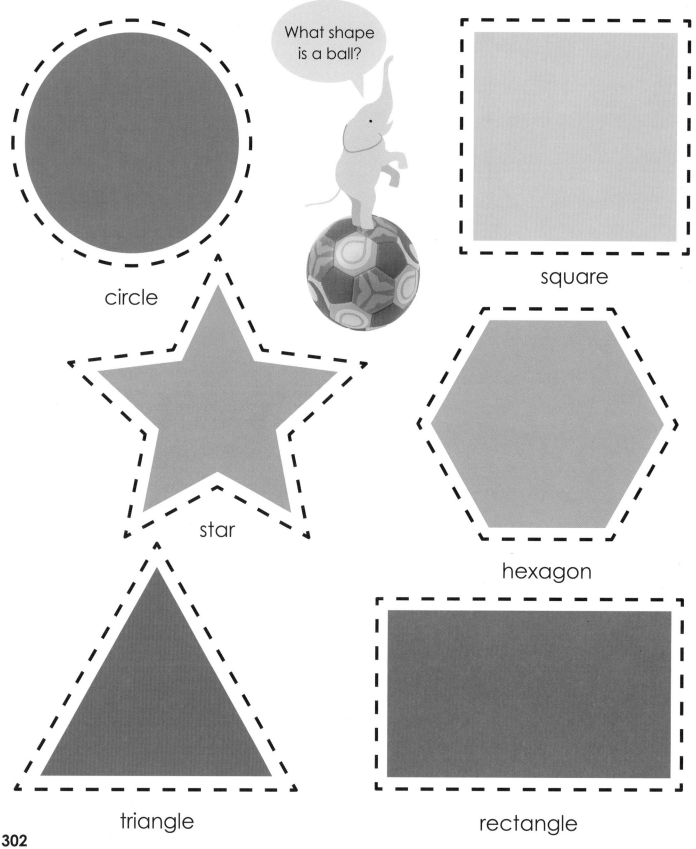

circle

What shape
is a ball?

square

star

hexagon

triangle

rectangle

Making shapes

Complete these shape pictures by tracing over
the lines and then copying the pictures.

triangle

party hat

circle

clock

square

picture

rectangle

Trace over
the words,
too!

chocolate

Matching shapes

Draw a line between each shape and
the object that matches it.

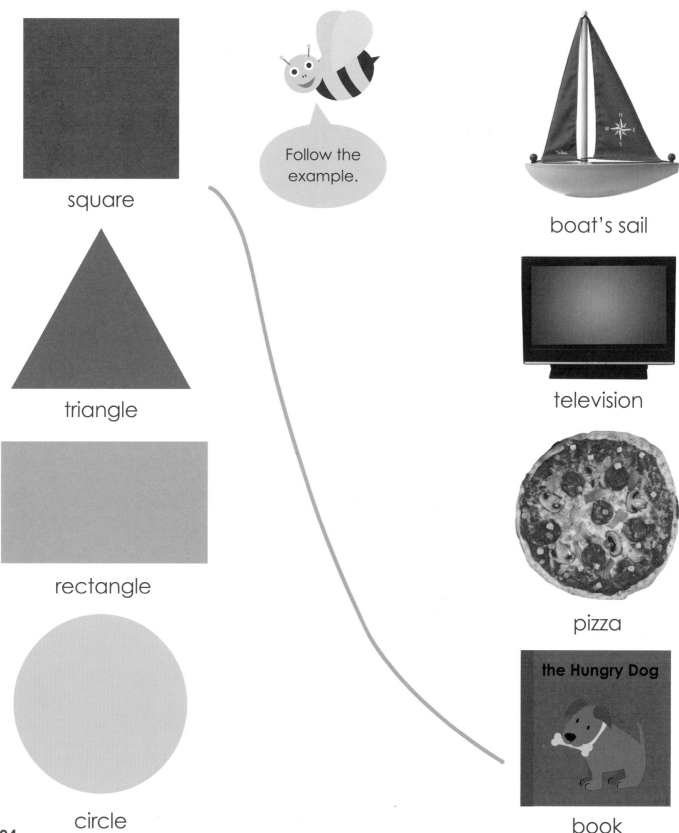

square

triangle

rectangle

circle

Follow the example.

boat's sail

television

pizza

the Hungry Dog

book

Shape patterns

Following the example, complete the shape patterns by drawing the missing shapes onto the spaces below.

Days of the week

What do you like to do during the week? Fill in the boxes using the matching picture cards at the back of this book.

Monday

On Mondays, I like to splash around!

Tuesday

On Tuesdays, I go dancing!

Wednesday

On Wednesdays, I stay indoors.

Ask an adult to help when cutting out the picture cards.

Monday

Tuesday

Wednesday

Days of the week

Can you say the days of the week?

Thursday

On Thursdays, I look after my pet.

Friday

On Fridays, I play outside.

Saturday

On Saturdays, I meet people.

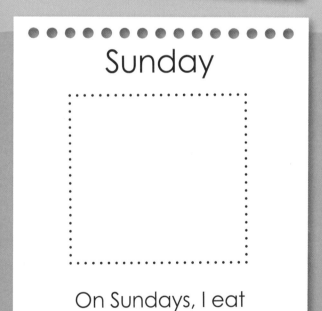

Sunday

On Sundays, I eat nice things.

Thursday **Friday** **Saturday** **Sunday**

Months of the year

What do you do in your year? Fill in the picture frames using the picture cards at the back of this book.

January

Valentine's Day

February

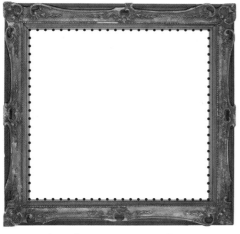

March

April

Buzzy Bee's birthday

Don't forget to trace over the words!

May

June

Months of the year

Can you see when it's my birthday?

July

August

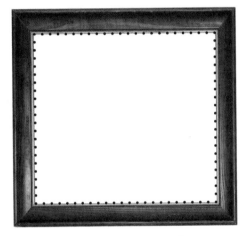

September

Halloween

October

November

Christmas

December

Weather match

Draw a line to match the weather pictures
with what you would wear outside.

snowy day

sunglasses

rainy day

gloves

sunny day

raincoat

Going away

Which items should you pack for a sunny vacation?
Check the boxes next to the things you should take.

Starting sounds

Draw a line between the letters and the
pictures that start with the same sound.

a

t

b

c

cat

apple

tree

ball

Say each
sound aloud
first.

Missing letters

Using the pictures to help you, fill in the missing
letters in each of the words below.

Cheep,
cheep!

n_st

j_mp

h_nd

t_nt

Rhyming pairs

Draw a line between the two words that rhyme with each other. An example has been done for you.

 clock

 can

 man

 cat

 hat

 sock

 log

 jar

 car

 dog

Missing rhymes

Each sentence is missing a rhyming word. Circle the correct one, then complete the sentence by writing it in the space.

The cat sat on the _____ .

| log | mat | chair |

The dog was on a log in the _____ .

| sun | fog | rain |

Can you see the bee in the _____ ?

Hello!

| car | house | tree |

At the toy store

Draw a line to match the coins to the toy of the same value.

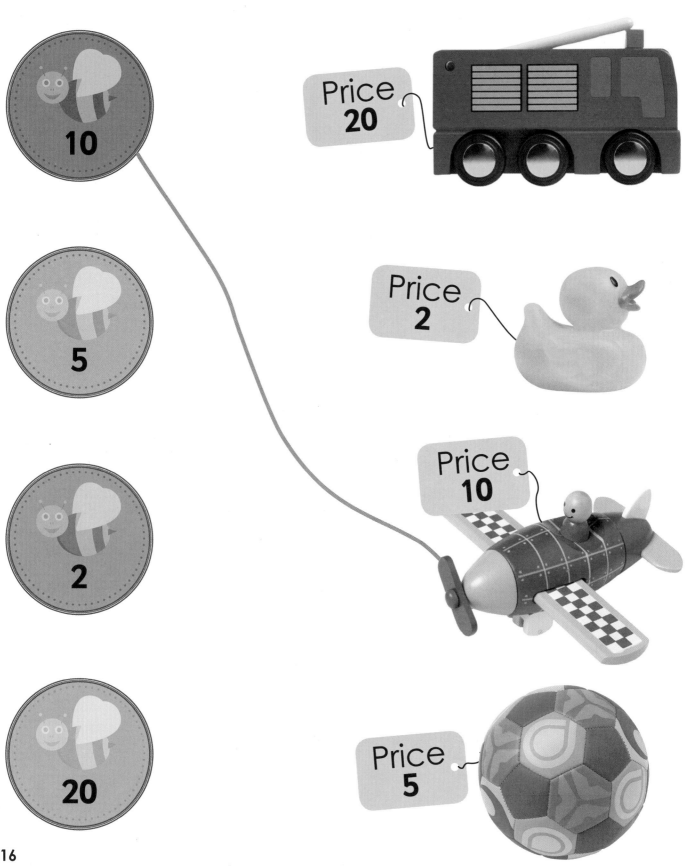

10

5

2

20

Price
20

Price
2

Price
10

Price
5

What can you buy?

Take each quantity away from 10.

You have 10 coin to spend.
How many toys can you buy?

10

Airplane
5

Duck
1

Doll
10

Truck
5

Balloon
5

Wand
1

Car
5

Fire truck
10

Teddy
2

How many  can you buy?

How many can you buy?

How many can you buy?

How many can you buy?

317

Day and night

Draw a sun or a moon in the boxes below to show the things you might see, hear, or do in the day or night.

day   night

You've reached the end of the book. Good job!

see stars in the sky

go to school

go to sleep

hear an owl

eat breakfast

fly a kite

Picture cards

Ask an adult to help you cut out these cards.

swimming lessons

do ballet

arts and crafts

walk the dog

play sports

visit family

bake day

Use on pages 306–309.

spring day

my birthday

let's celebrate

summer vacation

winter day

first day of school

camping

Easter

school play

sleepover party

zoo visit

fall day